THE BARKS & BEANS CAFE
MYSTERY SERIES

NO FILTER

THE BARKS AND BEANS CAFE MYSTERY
SERIES: BOOK 1

HEATHER DAY GILBERT

Series: Gilbert, Heather Day. Barks & Beans Cafe Mystery; 1
Subject: Detective and Mystery Stories; Coffeehouses—Fiction; Dogs—Fiction
Genre: Mystery Fiction

Author Information & Newsletter: http://www.heatherdaygilbert.com

FROM THE BACK COVER

Welcome to the Barks & Beans Cafe, a quaint place where folks pet shelter dogs while enjoying a cup of java...and where murder sometimes pays a visit.

Fed up with her go-nowhere job, newly single Macy Hatfield moves back to her small hometown in West Virginia. She joins forces with her brother Bo in his crazy new venture—the Barks & Beans Cafe, which caters to dog lovers and coffee drinkers alike.

When a golf instructor is murdered at the nearby spiritual center, Macy winds up adopting his Great Dane. Just after Macy finds a mysterious message sewn under the dog's collar, her Dane is dognapped. She launches into a relentless search for her newfound canine friend, but along the way, she digs up a cruel and confident killer.

Join siblings Macy and Bo Hatfield as they sniff out crimes in their hometown...with plenty of dogs along for the ride! The Barks & Beans Cafe cozy mystery series features a small town, an amateur sleuth, and no swearing or graphic scenes. Find all the books at heatherdaygilbert.com!

The Barks & Beans Cafe series in order:
Book 1: No Filter
Book 2: Iced Over
Book 3: Fair Trade

1

My nail polish matched the dirt outside my patio. I downed a long sip of sweet iced tea and wiggled my freshly painted toes. What had possessed me to pick up this "Burnt Mesa" shade anyway?

More importantly, what was I even *doing* in Starville, South Carolina?

I set my nearly empty glass down on the wicker table, making my hammock sway precariously as I eased back into it. I hated this kind of heat, the shimmering swelter of an unforgiving late August sun, but I hated air conditioning even more. I never seemed to be the right temperature in this state I'd settled in when I'd married my husband seven years ago.

Correction: EX-husband.

I'd discovered a bit too late that the seven year itch wasn't merely an amusing concept—Jake had cheated not once, but several times, and, in an Oscar-worthy performance, he'd announced that fact to me this past Christmas vacation. I'd been too blind to suspect him of it or even snoop into his texts, like my DMV coworker had suggested when I tried to justify why he was working late so often.

He'd walked out, forcing me to indefinitely cover the rent on our one-bedroom brick house.

The cicada whirr intensified, and I gave up at my attempt to relax on the patio. I rolled off the hammock before it could toss me over, something it seemed to enjoy doing.

My cell phone rang. I lazily glanced at the screen, then did a double take.

It was my brother, Bo. His given name was Boaz, but he never went by that. Another thing he never did was call me this time of day, since he logged long hours working as vice president at Coffee Mass, a wholesale coffee bean importer in California. I was a bit apprehensive as I picked up.

"Hey, sis," he said.

I heard hammering going on in the background. "What's up?" I asked. "Sounds like a construction zone there."

"It is," he said, and I could picture the crinkles fanning his sky blue eyes as he smiled. "Macy, I have some news."

I knew Bo had gotten engaged to his coworker Tara back in March, but given my freshly divorced status, I hadn't been as enthusiastic as I should've been. I tried to inject happiness into my tone. "Oh, yeah? Did you set a date?"

"What? Oh, no. I should've called you. The engagement is off." He fell silent.

My temper flared. "How—why—no girl in her right mind—"

"It wasn't entirely her fault," he said. "But that's not what I'm calling about. I actually made another decision last month." He hesitated.

My brother wasn't usually one to mince words. "Okay, and what was that?" I prodded.

He let out a breath. "Macy, I sold my shares and retired early. I'm back home."

I sank onto a chair, grabbing for my watered-down tea as if it were a lifeline. "You did *what?*" Talk about impulsive. Talk about letting someone derail your life.

"Oh wait, there's more." He chuckled. "I've got a business proposition for you...but the only stipulation is, you'd have to move back here. You think you'd be willing to do that?"

I rubbed my glass against my sweaty forehead, darkening my strawberry blonde bangs and plastering them against my eyes. I shoved them aside and tried to focus on what my brother was saying.

Would I be willing to move?

"Tell me more," I said.

Turns out, my brother, who had always been quite innovative, had decided to open a cafe in our hometown of Lewisburg, West Virginia. One half would be dedicated to coffee, hot drinks, and pastries, and the other half would feature a large area where customers could relax by petting rescue dogs.

"I couldn't stop thinking about our conversation at Christmas," he explained. "When I asked what job you'd do if you had all the money in the world, you said you'd want to work with dogs, because that made you the happiest. And you know how much I've studied coffee over the past ten years. I had the idea that we could meld our favorite hobbies together in a cafe."

"So you're saying this was all my idea?" I asked.

He laughed. "Sure, if you want to say so. Anyway, when I researched it, I saw that petting cafes aren't a new idea—in fact, they've really caught on in Asia and out West," Bo said. "Lewisburg would be perfect for it, since it's so close to The

Greenbrier Resort. We'd get the high-end clientele, as well as regulars who work in town."

He went on to explain that he'd launched a renovation on the front section of his inheritance—our great aunt Athaleen's house—and it was now a nearly finished cafe. He hadn't asked me to participate in that phase of his plan, because he knew I disliked all things remodeling.

Now the back section of Auntie A's was empty, and he thought it would be perfect if I could move in there so I'd be on the spot in case of any business emergencies. Besides, it was the house we'd grown up in, and he hated to rent it to anyone.

Since dogs had been my passion since childhood, he wanted me to handle the "Barks" half of the Barks & Beans Cafe—which I thought was a clever name for it. He could easily run the "Beans" half, with all his connections in the coffee bean world.

I glanced at the heat, shimmering off my blacktop driveway. I had a pleasant vision of digging in soil that was brown, not red. Of sitting on a back porch as a mountain breeze toyed with my hair. Of petting dogs all day long for my *job*. All my misgivings about moving back to the state where my parents died evaporated as I realized Bo had given me something to look forward to in my mundane life.

"I'm in," I said. And I knew I'd never look back.

"Let's take a look at the cafe again," I said, anxious for a breather from stripping floral wallpaper in Auntie A's dining room.

Bo glanced over from his side of the room. He rubbed at his red stubble beard. "You sure? This is a pretty big job, and I won't have as much time to help after we open."

"I'm sure." It was obvious my big brother had more endurance than I did, even though he was forty-one and I was only thirty-seven. I was ready to poop out for the day.

After giving a three weeks' notice with my job and my landlord back in South Carolina, I'd sorted and packed all my belongings, then moved back to West Virginia. I'd only been here a week, but I felt exhausted and ill-prepared to tackle even the smaller maintenance chores, like replacing burned-out light bulbs and aged-out appliances.

Bo obligingly pulled a keyring out of his pocket and walked over to the wooden connecting door that led us into the renovated front section of Auntie A's house.

I followed him in, taking in the cozy feel of the place, which was outfitted with a top-of-the-line stainless steel espresso machine that cost more than my used Honda had. The interior of the shop was delightful—not a trace of mass-produced kitschy decor. Bo had painted the exposed brick walls white, installed dark wood flooring, and had used rough-hewn wood for the rustic tables and coffee bar. He'd even built bookcases to line one wall. The cafe felt full of character and even comforting, somehow.

But the Barks section of the cafe was what thrilled my heart the most, since that was going to be my specialty. Rough wood divider walls and a gate separated the cafe from the petting area, allowing cafe-goers to see the dogs but still feel some privacy from them. The concrete floor in the dog area contrasted nicely with the warmth of the built-in benches, feeding areas, and dog toy bins. Bo had wisely added a side door leading to an outdoor fenced dog run, where pooches could attend to their bathroom needs.

I found myself envisioning the pups who would rotate through our cafe and wishing for one of my own. My rental house hadn't allowed pets, but I'd always had a dog growing up. Just one more thing I had sacrificed on the altar of Jake.

"You know, I think this place is perfect," I said, feeling a wave of appreciation. "You did a great job with it." I was secretly relieved Bo had already designed the place and gotten most of it set up before he'd asked me on board. That would have been a daunting task for me—too daunting, I suspected. I didn't like interior decorating, and I didn't have a natural sense of style, like most women seemed to. I'd be happiest meeting the employees and hanging out with the dogs.

My brother, who wore a tank top that showed off his tattoos, grinned at me. He'd been a Marine for seven years, and he still looked like one. I knew for a fact that he conceal-carried his Glock almost everywhere he went.

"I'm glad you think so. Auntie A would've approved, I think —we'll be helping dogs find homes, the same way she opened her home to us." He fell silent, probably still reeling from Auntie A's sudden death in January, just like I was.

Our great aunt Athaleen had adopted us when I was only two, after our parents died in a creek flood. She was kind of like a dad and a mom rolled into one. She knew how to fix the pipes in the basement and how to cook our favorite turkey dinner. She was an unmovable rock in times of difficulty, and a soft blanket when we were sick or sad. Bo was right—she would've loved what we were doing with her place. She'd likely say she was "proud we carried the Hatfield name," which had been a common refrain of hers.

Although late-stage ovarian cancer had stolen her health quickly, I couldn't stop wondering if Jake's Christmas betrayal of me had led to her death early this year.

I grabbed some paper towels and a bottle of cleaner, turning toward the paned front windows to hide my tears.

After spraying each section thoroughly, I started wiping the windows down. "When were you thinking we'd open?"

"I wanted to give you time to get settled in, but I already have people applying for jobs. I figured we could start interviewing tomorrow, if that'll work for you."

"That'll work." I went over a streak that didn't seem to want to disappear. "Hey, I'm not going to have to make coffee or anything like that, am I? You know I'm better at brewing tea than making coffee. And that espresso maker looks like it could chew my hand off if I handled it wrong."

Bo laughed. "I wouldn't get anything that could hurt anyone. But no, I don't expect you to make the coffees. I'm hoping to hire enough baristas so that we can rotate them out, then you can focus on the dogs."

"Could we get someone to stand in for me if I have to take sick days or anything?"

He slid coffee flavoring bottles into a wire rack. "Of course. I was planning on that. You wouldn't be doing this alone."

"You've thought of everything." I walked over and gave him a high-five.

"Let's hope so," he said. A shadow of doubt crept into his eyes, and I quickly turned away to hide my surprise.

My brother had never shown any doubts when he'd pursued his dreams before. What had Tara done to him?

2

My clothing for the interviews was eclectic, to put it mildly. I hadn't unpacked all my boxes yet, so I felt a bit shoddy, showing up in ripped jeans and a paint-splattered T-shirt.

True to form, Bo didn't even raise an eyebrow at my getup. And when the first job candidate came in, I actually felt a bit overdressed.

Kylie was on the younger end of twenty-something, wearing a midriff top that showed off her belly ring and quite a bit of a dragon tattoo that wrapped up her neck and down both arms. Her faded black jeans were so ripped up, they might as well be cut off and turned into underwear.

I asked her a few questions, to which she offered nothing more than curt answers. I shot Bo a look that said *Shut this thing down now*, but he must've misread me, because he took over the interview process. Kylie visibly softened and seemed willing to answer him, which made me wonder if she had some kind of serious mommy issues.

Still, she started to shine the moment he asked if she had any previous experience. She did—at a Dunkin' Donuts, where she'd innovated some of their coffee drinks and apparently made some lifelong customers, to boot. She'd studied coffee making techniques online, and she offered to make us each a drink of choice on the spot.

I took one sip of my caramel macchiato, complete with a foam dragon head floating on top of it, and I tossed my reservations out the window. This girl could brew a mean cup of joe, and the fact that she had loyal customers told me her coffee bar-side manner must be more engaging than her interview persona.

Bo and I went into the back room to chat a little, but returned quickly to tell her she was hired. She might be a tough nut to crack, but having her on the Barks & Beans team would be an asset in a trendy town like Lewisburg where customers appreciated edgy *and* delicious brews.

We hired three other workers, then Bo did a week of training with them on the espresso maker and register.

On Thursday, I placed a call to the owner of the local animal shelter, Summer Adkins. Her cooperation was essential to our cafe's success. Unfortunately, our conversation started out rough as I tried in vain to explain the objective of our cafe— to find homes for her shelter dogs.

"But what are you actually *doing* with the dogs again?" she demanded over the chorus of dogs barking in the background.

"They'll just hang out in the doggie section here at the cafe and enjoy getting loved on by customers. You'll choose which ones to bring. Of course, we'd want them washed up, deflead, dewormed, and vaccinated."

"People would be bringing their own dogs to the cafe, too? What about dog fights?" she asked.

"No. No outside dogs are allowed in. The idea is to focus on the shelter dogs."

Her tone was still irritable. "What if this cafe doesn't move dogs? Do people understand this isn't a no-kill shelter? Do *you* understand that, Mrs. Hatfield? That means dogs eventually wind up being euthanized if they're not wanted."

"It's *Miss* Hatfield, and yes, I totally understand." I took a deep breath. "Listen, Barks & Beans will help you out by allowing people to spend time with the dogs so they know they're a good match right up front. It can only result in more adoptions than you have now. It's honestly a win-win." Bo handed me a London Fog tea and I curled tighter into a booth, giving him a nod of appreciation and summoning more fortitude. "Summer, please understand that we're asking that people buy at least one beverage before entering the dog area, and we're going to give you a percentage of that cover charge to help with shelter expenses."

That seemed to shut her up, so I agreed to drop by later that afternoon to look over the dogs and talk logistics.

Bo took a break from arranging vintage classic books on the shelves. The library had donated several boxes of books when they'd heard we were looking for them. The head librarian and Bo had been in the same grade in school, and I suspected her bookish gift was intended to be more than just a friendly gesture. But Bo acted oblivious to the come-ons of women in town, which seemed to occur every time we went out.

Meanwhile, the *stay back* vibe I was trying to project didn't seem to be working, since every time I went to the grocery store or Walmart, random people struck up conversations with me. I wished I *could* be a little more oblivious.

My brother and I were like the walking wounded, and anyone who dared to attempt a relationship with either of us was likely to get burned.

SUMMER ADKINS WAS NOT REALLY what I expected from our phone conversation. I'd anticipated meeting an uptight, older sourpuss. But Summer was my age, had pale violet hair, and wore flowy pants and a leather vest-shirt that looked straight out of the Sixties.

As she took me on a tour of the facility, she asked, "What kinds of dogs do you want? Big, small, fluffy?"

"As long as they're not aggressive, we'll take any kind." I slowed by a kennel with a tiny dog that was jumping to get my attention. "We'll probably need four to five dogs a day, depending on what you have."

She gestured around the kennel area with her numerous turquoise rings. "As you can see, we have lots to choose from. Take your pick. The only one with behavior issues is that old Husky mix over there."

I peered in at the Husky mix and he gave a low growl. It was sad that his distrust of people would inevitably hinder his chances of being adopted.

Summer must've read the look on my face. "Tough cases, like this one, do sometimes get adopted. It just takes a lot of rehab type work. I'm surprised he's not barking at you." She came over and dropped a dog treat in his kennel, which he snapped up. He sniffed at the fencing, but I knew better than to try to pet him.

I chose six dogs to come in for our grand opening the next day. Summer agreed to transport them over early in the morning, then I'd take them back at the end of the day with Bo's heavy duty truck.

Cute as the dogs were, none of them really appealed to me, which was unfortunate. I'd been eagerly anticipating finding a doggie companion to share Auntie A's home with, since her old golden retriever Jasper had died just a month after she had. Dogs had always clattered up Auntie A's wooden stairs or woofed at strangers in her kitchen. The place seemed empty without one.

After reiterating that cafe customers who wanted to adopt would have to go directly to the shelter to fill out paperwork, Summer asked if I had any questions.

"Not really," I said. "Are you from around here? I don't think I went to school with you, did I?"

"No, I'm from Pennsylvania," she said. "I actually grew up Mennonite, if you can believe it." She pointed to her colorful hair and clinked her rings together. "I'm not anymore."

She walked me out to my red car and I shook her hand. "I'm looking forward to seeing you tomorrow," I said. "This is going to be fun."

To my surprise, she smiled. "You know what, Macy Hatfield? I actually believe it is."

When Summer dropped the dogs off at five thirty in the morning, she was able to meet Kylie as well as Jimmy, an older high school bus driver who'd wanted a change of pace. Kylie and Jimmy were covering the early shift. Bo was planning to come in when the place opened at six and supervise.

Summer seemed genuinely impressed with our petting room. She helped me walk the dogs around their play area and outside run, then she bought a coffee and headed out before the doors opened.

And once the doors opened, customers began to steadily trickle in. Bo was thrilled when he arrived and found we were already on the second box of pastries from Charity, our older baker who was raising her four year old grandson on her own.

The dogs were lapping up the attention and behaving themselves fairly well—Summer seemed to have chosen them carefully. There was a golden retriever mix that reminded me of Jasper. He must've sensed I liked him, because he stayed right around me.

By lunchtime, all the dogs were getting antsy, so Bo and I took turns taking them out to their run. Two tiny dogs started nipping at each other, but I was able to distract them and get them inside unscathed.

A couple of women in fashionable heels sat on a bench in the doggie room. The younger blonde woman squealed when I brought the little dogs in and surprised me by sweeping up the Chihuahua mix and plopping him onto her expensive skirt. She began to vigorously scratch behind his ears, and instead of nipping at her, as I'd fully expected, he rolled over and seemed to pant with delight.

"Oh, look, Mary Anne," she gushed to her friend. "Isn't he just the sweetest little thing?"

I was curious as to how this obviously high maintenance woman had such a rapport with dogs. She began speaking and didn't make any attempt to modulate her voice for the enclosed space, so her every word was loud and clear.

"Let me tell you, I've found a gem." Apparently I'd walked into the middle of an ongoing conversation, since her next words made it clear she wasn't talking about the dog in her lap. "A golf instructor who can explain how to play *without* sounding condescending, can you imagine? The last club we belonged to, I swear the instructor did nothing but talk down to me, like I was brainless."

Mary Anne murmured, "Oh, Isabella. It happens all the time, doesn't it?" She blew air kisses to the little mutt she'd awkwardly positioned on her lap.

Isabella continued. "Yes! Now listen, you've got to visit this place—the Ivy Hill Spiritual Center for Healing, that's the one. I know the name sounds kooky, but the golf course is gorgeous.

It's not as large as The Greenbrier of course, but I know you and Darren were looking for a more private place..."

Conversation trailed off as Kylie delivered coffee to the women, which was an event in and of itself. The posh socialites eyed Kylie's tight leather pants, leopard-print shirt, and combat boots. Then they looked down at their wide coffee cups, which bore delicate foam art representations of a peacock and a panda bear, respectively.

Isabella gushed over Kylie's work, and Mary Anne swore she'd never seen a more beautiful coffee, even in Italy. Kylie walked away with a wide smile on her ruby red lips.

Something good was happening at Barks & Beans—people from very different walks of life were bonding over coffee and dogs. A sense of pride washed over me to be a part of this business. There might be some good left in my life, after all.

As the women sipped their coffee, Isabella piped up again, and I realized she was still talking about her golf instructor. "His name is Gerard Fontaine, so be sure to ask for him. He's wonderful. Although he had an off day yesterday—he kept glancing around while I was practicing my swing. But I saw this tall woman walk by on the hill and that seemed to be what he was looking at. I think she's the masseuse there? Anyway, he got the strangest look on his face when he spotted her and really lost focus." She giggled, giving her pup's tummy a rub. "Of course, it wasn't hard for me to pull his attention back with my many charms."

Mary Anne laughed. I tossed a ball to the golden retriever mix like I wasn't listening, but now I was fully engaged in this conversation I wasn't even a part of.

"Although, come to think of it," Isabella continued, "Gerard was distracted the whole time I was there. When he took me to the director's office to pay, there was this weird tension between the two of them. I didn't know if it was attraction or dislike, you know?" She set the dog on the floor and took a long, thoughtful sip of coffee. "She had all this natural decor in the office—a bit gauche, you know? Like dried wood and seed pods and wooden vases."

Mary Anne made a face as the dog in her lap stood and started circling. After setting the pooch on the floor, she leaned in closer.

Isabella was on a roll. "You know what? When I got home, I realized one of those vases was carved—and it wasn't wood. Remember that glossy carved horn-looking thing at Christa Bell's art exhibition? They said it was a rhino horn. I could swear that's what the director had sitting on her desk, pretty as you please. That thing would be worth a fortune!"

Mary Anne gasped and began talking in a low tone, but another customer entered, so I introduced him to a friendly Sheltie mix that seemed to strike his fancy. The rest of the day seemed to pass quickly, and when Jimmy and I returned the dogs to the shelter at five, I was overjoyed to hear that one of them was going to be adopted the next day.

Two DAYS LATER, Charity and I were arranging baked goods on paper doilies in the glass case when she jabbed her finger at the local paper.

"Did you see the paper? Someone got killed not far from here—whacked on the head with a golf club and found face down in a shallow pond. Can you believe that? Drugs, most likely."

Everything was drugs in Charity's book, and I didn't blame her for thinking that way. Her son and daughter-in-law were users, which is how she'd wound up fostering her grandson.

As I skimmed over the story, Charity was still talking.

"Spiritual Healing Center, my foot," she said. "They're saying that golf instructor got killed with one of his own clubs. That's just flat-out cold, you know?"

My eyes caught on the name of the murdered golf instructor—none other than Gerard Fontaine, the man Mary Anne and Isabella were discussing here just a couple days ago. Did his death have something to do with the masseuse he couldn't stop looking at? Or maybe the center's director was somehow involved...didn't Isabella say things were tense between her and Gerard?

I shoved my suspicions aside and refocused on my work. The police would be looking into things, and Charity was right —it probably was a cut-and-dried murder involving drugs. Our state seemed helplessly trapped in a raging opioid and crystal meth epidemic.

The day seemed to pass quickly. My phone rang around two in the afternoon, and Summer was on the other end. "I have a dog I need you to pick up," she said. "We just got him. He's a purebred Great Dane, but I can't fit him in my car. I think he'd be perfect for Barks & Beans—he'll probably get adopted quickly. Could you come over today?"

I asked Bo to keep an eye on the dogs while I drove over to pick up the Great Dane. Summer was right—a purebred would likely be easy to place. I wondered how he'd wound up in the shelter.

Summer ushered me into the building and began to explain. "I have his purebred registration papers," she said. "He's a gorgeous dog—well-groomed and well-behaved. Given his clipped ears, I think his owner was going to breed or show him, but he also appears to have been fixed, so maybe that didn't work out."

I took one look at the huge black animal in the kennel. His mournful brown eyes, which were the color of light maple syrup, met and held my gaze. Although the other dogs were yipping away, he kept quiet. His glossy black ears stood at permanent attention, accenting the strong lines of his head.

"Why on earth would someone get rid of him?" I asked. "He seems so gentle, and he must be worth a lot."

"Oh, he is." Summer seemed to pause for dramatic effect. "His owner died." She leaned in closer and dropped her voice. "Murdered, in fact. Can you imagine? He was a golf instructor at that fancy spiritual center across town."

My skin prickled with goose bumps. "You mean the Ivy Hill Spiritual Center?"

"That's the one. A guy named Gerard Fontaine."

3

I DIDN'T HAVE time to ponder the irony that a murdered man's dog had wound up in the shelter. Summer and I had to fashion a makeshift ramp with a large piece of plywood, but we managed to get the huge dog into the back of Bo's white truck. I offered to sit with him and hold his leash while Summer drove us the short distance to Barks & Beans.

As the warm late-summer air swirled around us, the dog pressed his entire weight against me as if his life depended on our connection. I gave his enormous, sleek head a pat, and he nudged into my palm with his eyes closed, as if he could finally relax.

I considered what Summer had told me about the dog. Some guy had showed up last night saying he worked at Ivy Hill with Gerard. He said that since the Great Dane was an indoor dog, no one was willing to take him in because they didn't feel they had room in their homes.

Summer thought it was strange that the dog had been parceled out when they probably hadn't even read Gerard's will yet, but it made sense to me—dogs were the kind of property that needed immediate care.

By the time we reached the cafe, I had my arm firmly wrapped around the dog and he was looking at me like I was his rightful owner. As we helped him climb down, I asked Summer what his name was and she said "Coal." It was a perfect West Virginia name, and it suited the shiny black dog perfectly.

Since Coal seemed loath to leave my side, I reluctantly walked him directly into the petting section. I'd already made up my mind—this was the dog I was going to adopt, and I didn't really want to show him off to the world. Call it a coincidence or some kind of divine perfect timing, but Coal had instantly bonded with me, and I wasn't about to let him go.

Bo's eyes followed me as I entered with Coal, but he didn't say a word. I knew my brother recognized my possessive look and he wasn't about to ask why I'd brought this gigantic dog in.

Bo's gaze shifted to Summer as she strolled in, and it lingered on her a moment too long.

No way. Did my brother find Summer attractive? She was a far cry from the bossy, career-driven women he tended to favor.

Bo walked over and introduced himself, then asked Summer if she was a volunteer at the shelter. It was actually a compliment, because he obviously assumed she was younger.

She didn't take it that way.

"I happen to be the *owner*, Mr. Hatfield," she snapped. When she whirled back to me, her eyes were flashing. "My coworker texted that he's here to pick me up. I hope you'll be able to get Coal back to the shelter tonight, Macy. Let me know if you need help." She stalked toward the door.

I rushed over and grabbed her elbow. "Actually, I've decided to adopt Coal," I said. "I'll do the paperwork when I drop the other dogs off tonight."

Bo stared at the dog, who had plopped down at my feet and was giving him a dubious look. "You're—"

I cut him off. "We'll talk in a minute." I turned back to Summer. "I'll see you later."

Summer gave a short nod and headed out. Bo came over to my side and looked at Coal. "So you're really going to adopt this big guy? Is he trained? He's huge, sis. If he stood on his hind legs he'd be taller than you."

I ignored Bo's jab at my height—he was six foot one and, at my diminutive five foot three, I always felt a bit shrimpy standing next to him. Apparently, I took after my mom's long-distant Inuit side, although I looked anything but with my pale skin, light eyes, and fair hair.

"I can handle a big dog, Bo. Don't you remember Caesar? He was at least eighty pounds."

"I think this one far exceeds that weight class." Bo leaned down and gave Coal a once-over. Coal didn't budge from my feet, but he did give Bo's hand a cursory sniff. He then proceeded to give a broken-up growl that sounded less like a threat and more like he was trying to speak. He shoved his head up against Bo's palm and held it there, waiting to be petted.

Bo laughed. "Okay, sis. I can't argue with that. This dog is practically human, and he's obviously attached to you."

I hadn't told Bo that Coal had belonged to a murdered man, and I didn't intend to. Some things were better kept to oneself.

I TOOK Coal around to my section of the house so he could settle in before I had to head out again. Once I opened my door, he hesitantly stepped inside, then proceeded to give everything a good sniffing. I placed some dog treats in a bowl and set out a water dish. Coal seemed to find the place to his liking, plopping down near the couch with what sounded like a contented sigh.

As quickly as possible, I locked up the house, then went around and loaded the shelter dogs in Bo's truck. When I dropped them off, Summer helped me fill out the paperwork for Coal, making me his proper owner for an astoundingly low price.

Flooded with excitement that I finally had a dog to call my own again, I ran into Dollar General to pick up dog food. I got a little distracted by the dog toys and treats and purchased several for Coal, then I managed to snag the last oversized dog pillow from the top shelf.

By the time I got home, Coal was no longer in the living room. When I gave a shout, he trudged down from upstairs, looking sleepy. I jogged up to make sure he hadn't made a mess, only to find a warm area on my bed where he must've burrowed under the quilt I hadn't smoothed out this morning. He'd made himself at home, alright. Had Gerard let the huge dog sleep in his bed? That wouldn't work in my full-sized bed—Coal would take up the majority of it.

I placed his new pillow next to the bed, patting it so he'd come over and try it out. He seemed to consider it a moment, then gave me a look that was so pathetic I couldn't possibly stick to my guns. Instead, I walked downstairs, found my funky orange rubber boots, and called for him so we could take a walk in the garden. We'd figure out the sleeping arrangements later.

Auntie A always prided herself in her perennial flowerbeds, and with good reason. Over the years, she'd accumulated cast-off plants from neighbors and arranged them in ways that made the large back yard look like a paradise. Although the dry grass was blanched now at the end of summer, Bo had kept it mowed down so it formed soft pathways between the flowerbeds.

Coal tumbled out the door after me, anxious to explore the enclosed garden. I pulled a few weeds near the last of the purple phlox of the season, then, just because I could, I plunged my fingers into the rich dirt Auntie A had amended over the years. It felt good to be home.

After nosing into every corner of the garden, Coal tripped his way back to me and sat at my feet, anxious for some attention. I patted his head, then rubbed his chest and neck. He wore a brown leather collar that was quite stylish and, I imagined, quite expensive. How did a humble golf instructor afford such a collar, not to mention purchase a purebred dog like Coal?

I scratched the silky fur under the wide leather band and my finger caught on something protruding from the back of his collar. I unbuckled it and slipped it off his neck for closer inspection.

I was surprised to find an engraved metal tag stitched to the underside of the collar. It didn't appear to be a dog identification tag, since it said "Amber 457301." Coal was obviously *not* an "Amber."

Why would Gerard go to all that trouble to hide a tag this way? And what on earth did it mean? Maybe it was the phone number for a woman named Amber? No, it was a digit short for that, and even if it was, why bother hiding it so carefully?

I went into Auntie A's gardening shed and found a pair of scissors. After snipping the bothersome tag off, I shoved it into my pocket, then buckled his collar on again. Coal happily lumbered off to sniff out a new adventure, while I sat on a wrought-iron bench and watched yellowed oak leaves drifting toward the ground.

Who was Gerard Fontaine anyway? That Ivy Hill Spiritual Center must be rolling in the dough for him to afford such luxuries, or else he was independently wealthy. But in that case, why would he choose to be a golf instructor?

The air had actually gotten a little nippy, so I sighed and stood. Coal rushed to my side, as if he feared being left alone. I supposed he *had* been alone for an extended period of time, before Gerard's body was discovered. Had Gerard actually been killed on the golf course, then dumped into the pond?

I looked into Coal's light brown eyes, which seemed to be full of sadness.

Was it possible Gerard had been killed at home, maybe even in front of his Great Dane? It was probably unlikely, but the dog surely acted like he was grieving. He must've been quite close to Gerard. Dogs were capable of such incredible loyalty. I hoped Coal would find me worthy of his trust.

Coal and I stayed up late for an impromptu *Le Femme Nikita* marathon. I loved the original series with Peta Wilson, and Bo had bought me the first season on DVD this past Christmas. It turned out to be the one highlight of the holiday season Jake had ruined by confessing all his affairs before walking out on me.

The next morning, I managed to sleep in until nine since Jimmy had offered to handle the early morning doggie duties for me at the cafe. Coal woke me by bumping into my arm—he must've crept onto my bed once I'd fallen asleep. A dull knock sounded, and I realized someone was at my back door. Bo had the key, so it couldn't be him.

I yanked one of my dad's old Oxford shirts over my head—they were some of the only mementos Auntie A had kept, maybe because she was proud he'd been a dentist. With Coal at my side, I peeked out the back window and saw a tall blonde woman with a deep tan standing on my doorstep.

She was about to knock again when I opened the door.

"Hello?" It came out a question, my voice scratchy from sleep. Who was this woman and why was she on my doorstep this time in the morning? "Can I help you?" I prodded when she seemed at a loss for words.

She took a step back as if surprised at my gruffness. "Uh, yes. They told me this was your place—you're Macy Hatfield, right?" Her gaze shifted to Coal and she clasped her hands to her chest. "Oh, thank goodness he's here."

"Hold on—who told you this was my place?" Coal pressed against my leg.

"The woman at the shelter. She said you'd adopted Gerard's dog. I'm so glad he's okay."

I was going to have to have a little chat with Summer Adkins, handing out my home address to just anyone. It seemed to me that once a dog was adopted, that kind of thing would be more privileged information.

"Oh, please pardon me for not introducing myself. I'm Katie Givens—the masseuse at the Ivy Hill Spiritual Center for Healing." She teared up and pressed her fingers to the corners of her eyes. "Gerard and I were very close, you see. He would've wanted me to take care of his baby boy." She peered around me and made a smoochy sound to Coal. The dog gave a low rumble.

It wasn't a friendly rumble. He clearly didn't like her.

I pulled the door closed a bit more, effectively blocking Coal from her line of sight. "So, you and Blackie here were tight, too," I said, deliberately giving the wrong name for the dog. "Why didn't you keep him when they asked around at Ivy Hill? I heard there were no takers because he was too big."

She played right into my trap. "Oh, yes. Blackie is very

attached to me. Sadly, I was out for training the day the staff sent the email asking for a new place to situate him, and I only found out later they'd accidentally left my name off the list." She tried in vain to peer over my shoulder to the dog, then gave up and looked at me beseechingly. "I would've dropped everything to pick up my big sweet poochie poo."

When I didn't respond, she fumbled at her purse, withdrawing a checkbook. "I'm happy to take him off your hands, and I'll pay you extra for the expenses you've had," she said, beaming a tragic—and definitely false—smile at me.

I could feel my face freeze. "I'm not sure what game you're playing here, Miss Givens, but *Coal* here has been legally adopted." I emphasized his real name so she'd have no doubt I saw through her ruse. "He's not for sale. I'm sorry this was a waste of your morning." I slowly and firmly shut the door in her face.

I peered out the kitchen window to make sure she'd left, then I filled a kettle to make my morning tea. Coal trotted along behind me, so I refilled his water dish. Katie Givens wanted her hands on my dog for some nefarious purpose, I was sure of it.

Petting Coal's sleek forehead, I murmured, "Don't you worry, boy. You're safe now."

4

THE CAFE WAS in full swing by the time I headed over at eleven. I left Coal at home on his pillow I'd brought downstairs, planning to walk him on my lunch break.

As I opened the door, Milo, who I was certain was one of the most Millennial Millennials in town, looked me up and down. His eyes looked huge behind the thin lenses of his glasses, which I was pretty sure he'd only bought for fashion purposes.

"You're on fleek, hon."

I knew he meant it as a compliment—after all, I'd finally discovered the plastic tote filled with all my good work clothes, so I was rocking my slim black jeans and a French-chic camel colored sweater. I'd swept my hair into a loose chignon. But I was his boss, and I couldn't let him set a precedent of calling me *Hon.*

Before I could scold him, a young golden retriever broke away from the petting area and throttled past the cafe tables, nearly toppling one. In a brief moment of discernment, he slowed as he approached the wall, giving me an opportunity to loop my fingers under his collar.

Jimmy lumbered into the room. Flattening one large hand to his chest, he pointed at the dog with his other. "That one has been giving me fits today, Miss Hatfield."

I glanced down and nearly laughed. The dog's tongue was lolling out and he actually seemed to be grinning up at me, as if he were proud of his tiny revolution.

With fresh resolve, I said a firm "No" before walking the dog back toward the petting area. "I'll take it from here, Jimmy. If he keeps tearing off like that, we might have to call the shelter."

Jimmy gave a sigh of relief. "I'll clean up and help Milo, then."

Milo looked up from spraying whipped cream on top of a drink. "*Do* be sure you clean up thoroughly, Jimbo."

Jimmy didn't seem to mind the nickname, or maybe he didn't hear it as he walked into the back room, but I wheeled around. "Milo, please call the employees and the bosses by their actual names. I'm Miss Hatfield and this is Jimmy. Don't forget it."

Milo's face was nothing if not dramatic, quickly shifting from an expression of surprise to disdain to one of considered approval. Milo didn't need this job—at age twenty-seven, this was actually his *first* job since he still lived at home with his wealthy parents. Maybe we'd made a mistake in hiring him, but Bo and I had both been impressed with his verve for marketing the cafe, which included utilizing social media apps we weren't even aware of.

He adjusted his shirt collar and actually had the decency to look sheepish. "I'm sorry, Miss Hatfield. It won't happen again." He shot me a winning smile.

Bo walked in, carrying a fresh box of supplies. He slowed

and glanced around, as if picking up on the charged atmosphere. "Everything going okay?"

Milo shot a glance at my brother—more specifically, at my brother's large and straining biceps—and I hurried to put his mind at ease. "Everything's going well."

I looked down at the retriever, who had settled next to my feet as if he didn't have a care in the world, and hoped everything *was* going well. In my DMV job, I'd rarely exercised authority, but today it seemed to flow naturally. Maybe I was a little stronger than I gave myself credit for.

COAL COULDN'T GET to my side fast enough when Bo and I walked in for lunch. As Bo set to work making grilled ham and cheese on sourdough, I walked Coal out to the back yard. Recalling the metal tag I'd snipped off his collar yesterday, I realized maybe *that* was what Katie had really wanted, not Coal himself, although Great Danes could definitely be sold for a hefty price.

I had shoved the tag into my jeans pocket, I remembered. After urging Coal to hurry up with his business, we rushed inside. Taking the stairs two at a time, I charged up to my room and yanked the jeans out of my laundry basket. Sure enough, the tag was still in the pocket.

I tried to head back down, but Coal sat on the middle step, blocking me. I'd left the poor dog in the dust on my way upstairs, but now he wasn't about to let me get away.

"C'mon, boy," I said, edging around him. He tried to keep a respectful distance behind me as we made our way down, although he tripped and plowed into me as he missed the last step.

"Ouch!" I shouted, hitting the floor with my knees.

"Sis?" Bo yelled. "What's going on?"

"Nothing." I scrambled to my feet and walked down the hallway, grabbing my keychain from the transferware dish where I'd dropped it. I took it to the hall closet and turned on the flashlight on my phone. Getting down on the wooden closet floor, which caused Coal no end of consternation as he tried to divine my intentions, I leaned back, pushing at the back wall with both my feet. It gave, and a small, hidden panel opened, revealing my safe box. Moving Coal's wet nose from my face, I sat and opened it, dropping Coal's metal tag on top of my birth certificate, passport, and other valuable papers.

"Food's ready," Bo called. "Where are you?"

I shoved the box back into the hidden space. Coal began to whine and nudged into my hand, which made me drop my phone with the light down. After groping for the hidden panel, my fingers hit the edge of the small door, so I used my upper body to jam it closed.

"Sis?" Bo didn't like to be kept waiting when he made the effort to cook for me.

"Coming," I sing-songed, shushing Coal as I shut the main closet door.

Bo peered down the hallway at me. "What're you doing in there?"

I considered explaining the possible connection with Katie's visit and my consequent desire to hide Coal's tag, but that story would keep for now. As a child, I had let my imagination run wild, and I didn't want Bo thinking I was seeing things.

Though truth be told, I felt like my imagination had died the moment my ex's lies were revealed.

"Nothing important," I said, ambling over to the kitchen table. Bo situated an attractive plate in front of me. He had garnished the golden-toasted sandwich with a crisp pickle wedge, then added a bag of my favorite chips on the side.

I took the first bite, allowing the comforting flavors to hit me full-on. I sighed. "How could Tara give this up? You *did* cook for her occasionally, didn't you?" While I knew Bo hadn't lived with Tara, preferring to wait until after marriage for intimate relations, I also knew he couldn't resist cooking for those he loved.

Bo, who had already taken three bites to my one, stared at his plate. "Of course. Sometimes she stayed late and I'd bring her dinner."

I wanted to ask Bo all kinds of questions, but it was clear he was still unwilling to share much information. How would Auntie A approach this conversation with him?

She'd talk about herself, offering stories from her past to prod him into talking.

"You know how Jake ran around on me," I started.

Bo's head tilted up and his eyes met mine. Eyes that reflected a thorough disapproval of his wayward ex brother-in-law. His one-word response reflected it, too. "Yes?"

"I asked myself a thousand times if it was something I'd done wrong. Maybe I'd been lazy about cooking and ordered too much take-out. Maybe I hadn't been as supportive as I should've been. Maybe I'd let myself go a little."

Bo gave a fierce shake of his head. "No way, sis. It was nothing you did. Guys like that are jerks from the get-go; it just takes a while for it to become apparent."

"I agree," I continued. "That's the conclusion I finally came to, that it was nothing I'd done." I stood and walked over to the sink, putting water in the kettle so I could give Bo some space. "It's probably the same in your case, you know, with Tara. It wasn't anything you did, I'm sure."

My back was to him, but he didn't hesitate to respond. "It's not like that. It wasn't anything I'd done, just something she *thought* I'd done."

"Okay, that's clear as mud." I turned on the kettle and returned to my seat. I didn't want to see my brother's wounded look, but I forced myself to meet his eyes. I immediately wished I hadn't because his pain was so intense.

"Someone lied about me and said I was involved with her while I was engaged to Tara. This person deliberately torpedoed our engagement. I tried explaining that it was all a pack of lies to Tara, but she wouldn't listen."

"Why would she believe some random woman over you?" I asked, hoping he wouldn't clam up.

"Because the random woman produced ticket stubs and other receipts with my name on them to prove I'd been out with her on certain nights."

"What? How is that possible?"

"I haven't figured that out yet. I was just so embarrassed that this woman—a new coworker—was able to convince Tara that I'd been with her. You know I'd never cheat on a fiancée, sis. Or any girlfriend, for that matter."

"Of course not. It's ridiculous."

"I guess it's just a woman scorned and all that. I couldn't fight the accusations, and it got so awkward working closely with Tara that I decided to pull up stakes and head home."

Coal, who had snuggled into his pillow, lifted his head for a moment to offer a loud whine, then returned to his resting position.

Bo grinned. "Well, the dog's on my side, so I feel better."

"You know I'm on your side, too. Always."

Bo polished off his sandwich and dusted the crumbs from his hands. "Hey, let's you and I get out tonight. We've hardly done anything while we were setting up Barks & Beans, but they're having a chamber orchestra on the lawn outside

Carnegie Hall at seven—Bach, I think. Didn't you used to like Bach?"

I enjoyed a well-played harpsichord as much as the next girl, and the historic Lewisburg Carnegie Hall building was a gorgeous spot. Although it was doubtful they'd move a harpsichord onto the lawn.

"Sounds like a plan." I glanced at the clock as I stacked our plates in the sink. "We'd better get back to work," I said.

As if he understood English, Coal stood, stretched, and walked to my side, pushing against me for a final pet.

"How do you do that?" Bo asked, opening the door for me. "It's like you're communicating with him somehow."

I patted Coal's head, then told him to go sit on his pillow. He obediently marched off that direction. "I don't know, but dogs aren't stupid. They pick up on body language, tone of voice, all that."

Bo clapped a hand on my shoulder. "I'm glad we have you at the cafe, sis. You're perfect for this job. And I'm glad you've found a doggie friend."

Though his words were cheery, his tone was despondent. I wished I could erase everything that had happened with Tara. I wasn't sure when my brother was going to attempt dating again, but I had a feeling it wouldn't be anytime soon.

THE CONCERT WAS RELAXING, even without a harpsichord. When intermission came, a tall man with black-framed glasses and a devilishly strong cleft chin strode toward us. The tips of his tousled brown hair touched the jaunty scarf he had twisted around his Oxford collar, and he'd topped this look off with a tweed jacket. The overall effect was one of bookish masculinity.

My brother pushed up out of the lawn chair and reached out to shake the man's hand. "Dylan! Good to see you." He turned and gestured to me. "And this is my sister, Macy. She liked those prints you chose for the cafe."

I stood. "Oh, this is the art gallery owner you were telling me about?"

The man, who smelled a little like woodsmoke, gave a slight nod as he leaned my way and nodded. "Yes, I'm Dylan Butler—my art gallery is called The Discerning Palette. I'm glad you liked those prints."

"Well, if left to my own devices, I wouldn't have picked Redon prints for that space." Noting his startled look and realizing how rude I'd sounded, I placed a hand on his arm and rushed to continue. "But I'm so glad you did! Somehow they pull out muted colors in the interior and they add a touch of whimsy, which is perfect for a doggie cafe."

Dylan's raised eyebrows returned to normal and his voice held a note of appreciation. "You know your artwork."

"I minored in art history in college," I said. "It hasn't really come in useful, though. I have no artistic skills of my own. I just like to admire beautiful things."

"What did you major in?" he asked, stepping closer as the orchestra began to warm up.

"Broadcast journalism," I said, somewhat under my breath.

The music started and Dylan gave me a look I couldn't quite decipher before he whispered goodbye and headed back to his seat. Maybe he wondered how I wound up working at a doggie cafe instead of being an anchorwoman on the news. Shoot, it was a question I'd asked myself often enough.

The bitter truth was that I'd had a bit of a breakdown after college. It was like the tragedy of my parents' early deaths by a stupid, random flood finally hit me in one swelling blow. The breakdown derailed my confidence...and probably left me wide open to the eventual advances of one Jake Hollings.

I glanced over at Bo, who was gazing off into the distance as the music wafted around us. We were like orphaned Lost Boys, with no parents to tell us which people would prove dangerous to our psyches or which paths we should avoid.

Barks & Beans was a grand experiment for both of us, and it simply had to work. Not because of the monetary investment Bo had made—he'd assured me he didn't lack for money after selling his Coffee Mass shares. No, it needed to work because neither of us could return to the lives we'd had before. We needed to blaze a new trail and follow it without looking back.

5

Bo and I decided to walk home, since the evening air had shed its humidity and carried a chilly promise of fall.

I shrugged into my sweater. "Dylan seems interesting."

Bo turned to me, an unreadable expression on his face. "You like him." It wasn't a question.

"I'm not sure. He just seemed eclectic somehow. And knowledgeable. Also nice."

"He is knowledgeable, and he was very easy to work with. I didn't want to pay a lot for cafe artwork, but he caught my vision and steered me in the right direction."

I nodded and fell silent. It was the magic hour in Lewisburg, that time when the birds were chirping, traffic was slowing, and a hazy yellow glow fell on everything. The cozy smells of burgers on the grill drifted from outdoor dining areas, making my stomach growl.

Opening the gate to my back garden, I brushed into one of Auntie A's white rosebushes and got pricked. I took a closer look and realized one of the long stems had been broken since the time we left.

"That's weird. The wind wasn't bad tonight," I said. "Did you break that stem earlier?"

Bo shook his head. "Nope. I steer clear of those rosebushes. All those years of push mowing this yard taught me a thing or two."

A strange misgiving seized me and I hurried up to the back door and unlocked it. Coal wasn't sitting on his pillow in the living room, so I gave a short whistle. Picking up on my unease, Bo walked down the hall to the wooden connecting door, unlocked it, and gave the cafe a once-over. I stood in the middle of my living room, waiting for Coal to come clattering over to me.

Only he didn't.

I scurried around, calling for Coal as I checked all the downstairs rooms. By the time Bo finished his perusal of the cafe, I had gone through my second story and was pounding back to the kitchen.

"He's gone," I said, disbelieving.

"Did he get out?" Bo glanced around. He walked into the living room, where I'd left a window open.

My breath caught when I realized the screen had been shoved out.

"He must've escaped this way," Bo said. "I'll go look for him."

I trailed after my brother in a stunned daze, trying to understand why Coal, who had bonded with me so quickly, would've made a break for it. Had he been worried because I'd left him alone? Had he come looking for me? Or had he hoped to get back to Gerard's place?

As I mechanically shouted for Coal and combed the back garden, another possibility jumped to mind. Although my back door had been locked, what if someone had climbed *in* through that window and taken Coal? It was a long shot, but Katie had seemed dead-set to get her hands on him. The screen was lying on the ground under the window, but it was in pristine condition. Wouldn't the frame have bent or the screen have been mangled if a Great Dane had thrown its weight into it?

I explained my concern to Bo, so he slid the screen back onto the tracks to test my theory. I ran inside and shoved into it with all my might, and to my dismay, it did give in the middle and pop right out.

"It's an old window, and the new screen doesn't fit entirely flush." Bo slid it into place once again and gave me an apologetic look. "It seems like Coal did make a break for it."

Darkness had fallen by the time we had canvassed the whole neighborhood, and there was still no sign of Coal. While Bo fixed taco bowls for a hasty meal, I called Animal Control and reported Coal missing, just in case someone turned him in.

After I'd reluctantly nibbled at my food, Bo gave me an apologetic hug and headed home, leaving me to wallow in my loneliness.

I stayed up late, pulling the few pictures I had of Coal off my phone and designing missing dog flyers to distribute tomorrow. Coal had loved me instantly, so I refused to believe he'd run off. No, something else was going on.

KYLIE AND CHARITY were equally distressed to learn my dog had gone missing. Kylie said she'd make sure to hand each customer a flyer, and Charity went outside and posted flyers at other businesses on our street.

Summer barged in, trying to maneuver four dogs on leashes. She gave me a smile, then sobered as she saw my face.

"What's wrong?" she asked.

"Bo and I went to a concert at Carnegie Hall last night, and while we were gone, Coal escaped out my window—at least I think he did." I twisted at the dishrag I'd been using to wipe down the coffee bar, even though it hadn't needed it. "I'm a little worried that someone stole him. We looked everywhere and he didn't show up."

"Oh, Macy!" She walked the hyper dogs into the petting area and unleashed them. They promptly set to work sniffing each other, as well as their new environment.

For once, I didn't even feel like being around dogs. Although I'd only owned Coal a short time, I'd already bonded with him. I missed my dog, and I wanted him back.

Summer grabbed a handful of flyers. "I'll definitely put these up at the shelter. And I'll post them everywhere I go, too. Why do you think someone stole him?"

I put my hand on my hip, suddenly remembering what Katie said on my doorstep. "I meant to talk to you about that. Did you tell that masseuse from Ivy Hill where I lived? Katie something-or-other?"

"Oh, yeah, you're talking about the blonde, right? Katie Givens? She came in and said she had something she needed to tell the dog's new owner. I gave her your phone, but she made it sound like something urgent Gerard had been really nitpicky about as far as Coal's care, and she insisted on getting your address. Sorry about that. I meant to tell you she might drop by, but things were busy that day."

I wanted to ream her out, but she gave me such a penitent look, all my irritation was defused. "It's okay; I probably would've done the same," I admitted. "It's just that she showed up acting like Coal should rightfully go to her, but Coal was growling and obviously disliked her. She was trying to convince me how tight she'd been with Gerard and his dog, but I wasn't buying it. It just seemed really suspicious, you know?"

Bo walked in the front door, and like me, he was sporting dark circles under his eyes. "No luck finding the dog?" he asked.

I shook my head, choking up a little. I could mask my emotions with other people, but my brother could see straight into my heart.

Summer patted my back in a motherly way. "We'll find him," she promised. "I'll get the word out."

Bo gave me a brief hug before walking behind the coffee counter. "How about a mocha, sis?"

I nodded. Kylie shimmied aside, giving Bo space to brew our early morning java.

Summer's side-angled purple ponytail bobbed as she glanced at her phone, then shot a covert glance at Bo under her dark lashes. "Well, I'd better get going." She rolled the flyers up in her hand and turned toward the door.

Surprisingly, Bo responded directly to Summer. "See you later. I'll bring the dogs back to the shelter tonight." He turned back to me. "That will free you up to look for Coal if he's not home yet."

I wished I could go out immediately, but I was going to do my part to keep this business running. Taking the mocha Bo offered, I blinked back my tears and trudged toward the dog petting area. It was going to be a long day.

Just as I was about to head out for lunch, Kylie motioned me over to the counter. She gestured to a lanky guy who was waiting for his order at the end of the coffee bar. He was unconventional, to say the least, as the lower half of his head was shaved and the top sported a short Mohawk. His light brown clothes resembled a loose fitting potato sack.

"This dude was wondering if he could advertise here for a class he's teaching," Kylie said. "Up at Ivy Hill. Bo's already on break, so I told him to ask you."

I walked over to the man as Kylie turned back to her coffee prep. "Hi, I'm Macy Hatfield. Kylie said you were interested in advertising here?"

Instead of shaking my hand, his eyes met mine and he stared at me like he was lasering into my brain.

"Could I help you?" I didn't relish any more drama today. He needed to get this show on the road so I could get back to my place and decompress a little.

He gave a slight jolt. "Sorry, I'm one of those people who takes a minute to get a read on new acquaintances. My name's Jedi Ward—and yes, that is the name my mom gave me." He gave a chuckle and I smelled cigarette smoke on his breath. "If you wouldn't mind, I'd like to drop some papers here inviting people to my new class. It's a healing drumming class." He gave me a long look. "Maybe you'd like to come?"

I accepted the papers he offered and glanced over them. "Healing drumming? What's that?"

"Releases energy," he explained, taking the green smoothie Kylie handed him. "And it can help you access the next spiritual plane."

That sounded like the last thing I wanted to do—I had enough problems to deal with in this plane. "Uh, sure. We can put these out." We needed to establish rapport with other local businesses, and maybe Ivy Hill would let us put up flyers at their place sometime.

Jedi took a long sip of his green drink and nodded. "Great. The class starts at seven tonight, and the first one is free, if you decide you want to drop by." He peered at me closely. "If you don't mind my saying, I think it would help you relax. I can see the tension in your forehead."

I *did* mind him saying—after all, who was to say he wasn't mistaking my first forehead wrinkles for tension?

"Sure, I'll think about it," I lied. "Thanks for dropping in." I wheeled around and headed out the front door, since I didn't care to open the connecting door between my part of the house and the cafe. I liked keeping the curtain drawn on my own personal side of things.

The first thing I saw as I pushed open my back door was Coal's pillow, sitting unused in its corner near the couch. I turned away and went into the kitchen to fix myself a bowl of Ramen, something quick and easy so I could look for my dog again. Had my new dog really left me? Or was he out there somewhere, scared and wondering why I hadn't come to get him?

I hastily finished my noodles and walked outside. Examining the flowers closely, it seemed the only one that had been damaged was the rosebush, which was right next to the gate. The gate would've been easy enough for Coal to jump, but it seemed he would've crashed into more flowers on the way over.

My eyes traveled to the dirt next to the gravel pathway. It was dry, but there were obvious marks where something had dug in and ripped into the flat surface. I was fairly certain we hadn't torn up the dirt when we moved the furniture in.

The picture was becoming clearer for me. I was becoming more and more certain that someone had taken Coal—either by pulling him out the window or by enticing him with treats. They'd left the screen on the ground so I'd think the dog had escaped. Then they'd leashed him and walked him toward the back gate—where I was betting he'd dug in his heels and balked. They'd likely pulled on him, which caused him to dodge into the rosebush and snap a twig.

Was it time to call the cops and not just Animal Control? Did cops actually intervene in dognappings, or did they just expect the owner to put up the missing flyers and try to find the dog on their own? Of course, they'd search local shelters, but

Summer would tell me immediately if she heard Coal showed up. He wasn't an easy dog to miss.

No, I needed to follow the trail myself, and I had a feeling I knew where it would lead. An opportunity had presented itself, and although healing drumming wasn't something I would have ever chosen to do, if it got me closer to Ivy Hill and to Katie, the possibly thieving masseuse, I'd do it.

6

I DROVE by several store windows and telephone poles plastered with my missing dog flyers on the way to Ivy Hill. There hadn't been a single call with a sighting of Coal. I'd even scoured Great Danes for sale on the internet to see if someone had posted him, but I'd come up empty there, too.

I could've asked Bo to come along with me as backup, but he didn't really seem to buy my theory that Coal was dognapped. Maybe if I got some kind of proof that Coal was at Ivy Hill, Bo would come with me to my next class.

As I pulled onto the grounds of the spiritual center, my attention veered to a small pond where abandoned police tape was flapping in the breeze. It had to mark the spot where Gerard was killed. I shuddered to think of someone committing such a bloody crime, but I could easily visualize it. Someone had likely come over to talk to Gerard about golf, maybe casually leaning on their golf club. Then perhaps they had picked up the club and toyed with it, then *wham*, brought it down full force on poor Gerard's head.

After I rounded a wide curve, the spiritual center came into view. Both sides of the Tudor style house had been added onto, and now it seemed to sprawl like a dark bear crouching on the hilltop. The house appeared to have elbowed out all the trees, and the yard was bare except for the meticulous landscaping out front, which surrounded a gurgling fountain.

I walked toward the oak front door, taking a final glance over my workout gear. I'd chosen my nicest pair of yoga pants and a shirt that boasted an expensive logo, hoping I looked like I belonged at the place.

No overhead lights blazed inside the entryway—instead, battery-operated candles and twinkle lights cast a peaceful glow over the space. I felt my shoulders relax. Maybe this wasn't going to be so bad after all.

A teenager manned the front desk, so I asked her about joining the healing drumming class. She signed me up and pointed me down the long hallway.

When I came across the door with a paper marked "Drums" in barely visible pink highlighter ink, I opened it and stepped inside. The atmosphere in the room was thick with incense and candle smoke, and a small circle of people sat on the floor, each holding drums. Jedi, who was barefoot and had combed his Mohawk down, padded across the thick carpet to me and handed me a drum as attendees created space for me.

"You're welcome to remove your shoes." His voice was barely above a whisper. "We shall begin momentarily. I'm so glad you came, Macy."

I pulled off my shoes while glancing at the people situated around me. They looked mostly middle aged, like me, although there was a white-haired couple who sat with their legs crossed, like they were pros at this gig. Maybe they'd already accessed a higher plane, because they seemed quite mellow with their eyes closed and their faces tilted upward.

Jedi gently cleared his throat and cracked his knuckles, which made me cringe. Auntie A had always scolded us thoroughly when we cracked ours, swearing it would give us arthritis someday.

He tapped lightly on the drum as he launched into a full-blown explanation of brainwaves. At his signal, we joined him in a synchronized drumming effort. Jedi worked his way up to a pounding beat intended to guide us on a journey to the imagined center of the earth, from which we were to emerge in a different dimension. But with all the reverberating thumping, the migraine that had been threatening since supper time decided to engage full-force.

I placed my drum on the floor and backed out of the circle. Jedi had his eyes closed, so I slipped out of the room with no fuss.

Since I always kept an extra migraine pill in my pocket, I popped one. My headache had given me an opportunity to explore the center. I edged further down the hallway and peeped out at the front desk. As I'd suspected, the teen had gone home, since we were probably the only class of the evening.

The drums were still pulsing, but as I crept up the stairway, I stopped short when a dog bark sounded from upstairs. It was muffled, but it was decidedly deep, so it could easily be Coal. Since he hadn't really barked in earnest at my house, I wasn't sure if it was him, but it *could* be, and that was enough to propel me up the steps with lightning stealth.

I went from door to door, but all was silent until I got to a door marked *Doctor Mark Schneider*, where voices were murmuring inside. I turned in a circle, listening, but the hallway was otherwise silent. Had I simply imagined the dog bark?

The doctor's room door burst open, so I hastily moved

toward the stairs. Turning back for a quick glance at who was behind me, I caught sight of a woman with an impeccably made-up face, fitted dress, and heels. I realized it was Isabella, the woman who'd been discussing Gerard's golf instructing skills at our cafe.

I slowed at the top step and faced her. "Hello."

Isabella hesitated, then looked at me closely. "Oh, you're the woman from the doggie cafe, aren't you?"

I nodded. "Macy Hatfield. My brother and I run the place."

She gave a wobbly smile. Her eyes and nose were a bit reddened under the makeup, as if she'd been crying. "It's delightful. I keep trying to talk my husband into visiting with me, but he's not a dog person." She gave a slight giggle. "Or a cafe person, for that matter." She extended a hand. "I'm Isabella Rhodes. It's nice to meet you, Macy. Are you a regular at Ivy Hill?"

I shook my head, perhaps a bit too vociferously. "I'm just visiting—I wanted to try the drumming class, but I got a headache, so I was looking for a water fountain or something."

She gave me a knowing nod. "I tried that class—not for me, either. But there are water bottles in the mini fridge downstairs. Just go to the end of the hallway."

"Thanks," I said.

"Sure." She fingered the chain strap on her purse. "Don't let that class throw you. Jedi's kind of a wannabe, and not the most gifted teacher. But there are plenty of qualified people working here, like Doc Schneider." She jerked a thumb toward the door she'd just come from. "He's a fantastic psychologist."

Like a teakettle about to whistle, Isabella seemed ready to burst with her insider information. Even as I heard the drumming class dispersing downstairs, she touched my arm and lowered her voice.

"My golf instructor Gerard died suddenly, you see. You probably heard about it in the news. I needed to talk with someone about it. Unpack the grief, you know?"

I nodded, unsure where she was leading the conversation.

"I talked to the center director about it—Alice Stevenson. Have you met her? Anyway, I told her I needed some free therapy sessions since the murder happened on their property, to *my* poor golf instructor. She agreed to three sessions, and I've found Doc Schneider to be so understanding, about the death and other things."

"That's good." I wasn't sure if that was the appropriate response to someone discussing their free therapy sessions.

Isabella rolled right along. "At first I thought Alice was odd, but it seems she's quite kind. She assured me that all the golf students will be reimbursed for the lessons we're missing until she finds a replacement instructor."

As the chatter from downstairs seemed to drift closer, I interrupted Isabella's monologue. "Did you by any chance hear a dog barking during your session?" I asked.

She looked thoughtful. "Actually, I think I did! It was right when we were discussing my mother-in-law. I heard a couple of big woofs, but then Doc Schneider turned on his indoor waterfall so I could refocus. Why do you ask?"

Before I could answer, Jedi came bounding up the steps, his bare feet sinking into the carpet. "Macy," he gushed. "You abandoned us! What happened to you?"

Perhaps sensing she was no longer the focus of attention, Isabella said goodnight, sidestepping Jedi to head downstairs.

"I'm afraid I got a migraine. I had to look for some water."

"There's some in the—"

"I know, Isabella told me, thank you." I walked down the stairs, Jedi close on my heels. "I don't think I'll be doing your class anymore—I'm sorry. I just can't handle the drumming. But are there any other classes I could take?" I needed to keep up a pretense so I could locate the source of the dog barks.

Jedi was obviously peeved. "Well, not really—I mean, not on the same days."

"Any day is okay." I tried to sweeten my tone. "I could *really* use any kind of help while I'm working through my divorce."

He sighed and kicked at the carpet. "There is one class on Wednesdays and Fridays—it's the Thrive at Life class. I don't think it's as helpful as the drums for realigning your spirit, though."

"I'll just have to make do, I suppose. Could you sign me up?"

AFTER JEDI reluctantly signed me up for the class, I strode out into the brisk air, appreciating the planets and stars that now dotted the darkened night sky. I took a moment to pick out Cygnus the swan, one of my favorite constellations.

I was just about to round the front of the building to see if I could find an easy way to climb to the second floor when a security guard emerged from the shadows.

"Excuse me, miss. The parking lot is the other way."

I felt like an idiot and was glad he couldn't see the blush creeping up my cheeks. "Oh my word, it's been *such* a long day and I was just stargazing—it's such a great view up on the hill. Thank you so much."

I turned and strode back toward the parking area. So much for hunting Coal down tonight. But I'd be back tomorrow evening, and I'd make an excuse to go upstairs. I needed to make sure it was Coal before I called it in as a dognapping, otherwise word would get around town that an owner of Barks & Beans had a screw loose.

However, if someone had stolen my dog, I was going to make them rue the day they'd assumed Coal would be an easy target. Coal now came with strings attached—and those strings were attached to *me.*

7

THE NEXT MORNING, Bo asked how the hunt for my dog was going. He'd gone out looking for Coal after he closed up and wondered why he hadn't seen me out searching, too.

I hedged a little, telling him that I'd followed up on a possible lead outside town, but it hadn't panned out yet. I did plan to have a discussion with Bo about why I felt Katie had taken my dog and maybe even hidden him at Ivy Hill, but the cafe was busy, so I decided to hold off until after work.

Charity and Milo were bustling behind the counter. Always one to ply me with her baked goods, Charity offered me a thickly frosted caramel macchiato cupcake. Unable to exert any self-control, I gobbled the cupcake before heading back over to the doggie section, where we weren't allowed to have food.

Summer had dropped off a fairly sedate crew of dogs today. There was an older beagle, who occasionally launched into an impromptu, lonesome howl, as well as a couple of low-energy smaller dogs. It hit me that since we were matching customers with poochie pets, the number of dogs at the shelter might dwindle. It was a great problem to have, but at some point we might have to pull from shelters in neighboring towns.

I glanced toward the coffee bar when I heard a familiar voice. Isabella had come in alone, and she was placing an order for a low-fat, sugar-free vanilla soy latte. I had to smile, because she added one of Charity's irresistible cupcakes to her otherwise low-cal order.

She caught a glimpse of me and gave an excited wave. "Macy! I'm so glad to see you again!"

Milo gave me an inscrutable look from behind his glasses, but I was pretty sure he was curious as to how I would've befriended a country clubber like Isabella. Chances were, his parents ran in the same circles.

Isabella tottered over toward the doggie section in her elegant nude suede heels, stopping short at the divider wall. Since she didn't appear to have a job, I couldn't fathom why she felt the need to don designer heels every time she went out in our small town. If I were posh and wealthy, I'd wear slippers around and send my butler to pick up the coffee and pastries for me. Bo called it my "youngest child syndrome," and it was true—I loved being babied every chance I could. Jake had known that from the get-go, and had wooed me with expensive restaurants and elaborately planned activities.

Isabella leaned on wooden ledge, watching the dogs as she took a huge bite of her cupcake.

She closed her eyes. "Follow your bliss, honey. That's what I'm going to do."

I didn't know if she was talking to me or to herself, so I gave the dogs head pats all round.

After devouring her treat, Isabella focused on me. "I'm so glad I ran into you last night. I just feel like I need to talk to someone about the whole thing with Gerard. I mean, Doc

Schneider's helpful, but he's so...noncommittal, you know? Just like a shrink." She laughed.

I didn't mind exploiting her need to talk. After all, Gerard's death had to be connected with his Great Dane's dognapping, didn't it? It was entirely possible the dognapper was looking for the metal tag on Coal's collar. They hadn't gotten it, though—I'd checked my safe and it was still there.

"I understand," I said, wondering what fresh news Isabella might have today. She seemed to be a wealth of information, and she had no hesitation in sharing it.

"Gerard and I were so close," she began, taking a sip of her latte. "I haven't really shared this with my other friends, but Gerard told me he thought someone was stalking him. One night he saw shadows when he was locking up, and another time he was convinced someone had rifled through his stuff when he was out on the course." She sniffed. "I told him it must be his imagination. And now he's dead! I shouldn't have brushed him off like he was seeing things."

She did, indeed, seem to be grieving the loss of her golf instructor—perhaps a bit too much, if he was *only* a golf instructor? The beagle started whining, perhaps picking up on the sad vibes emanating from Isabella.

"I'm sorry," I said. "Did he feel anxious about any particular person he worked with? I mean, did anyone have a reason to stalk him?"

"No, everyone seemed to like him. I think he'd had a little tiff or two with the director Alice, but nothing too intense."

One of the smaller dogs strained at its leash to get to Isabella. "Do you want to pet one?" I asked.

"Of course!" She placed her almost-empty coffee cup on the table and pointed. "How about that fluffy one—do you think it's part Maltese?

I glanced down at the long-haired white dog. "I suppose it's possible," I said. Anything was possible, but I was doubtful this cutie had any strain of purebred in it.

Isabella walked over and took the small dog's leash before returning to our conversation. "For the past couple of years, Gerard hosted a Christmas party for the Ivy Hill staff and select clients at his house. It was the quaintest little home, over in Fairlea, and it wasn't far from the spiritual center."

I thought about confiding that Coal might've tried to return to Gerard's house so Isabella would give me the exact address, but I decided against it. Instead, I asked, "You said his house is quaint—is it similar to others in that area?"

"Oh, no." She gave a fond, reminiscent smile. "It's this bright yellow cottage and it has the cutest white gingerbread trim...in fact, it reminds me of a little gingerbread house with its sloped roof. It's over on Third Street." As she scratched at the white dog's ears, it nuzzled into her hand. Was Isabella ever planning on adopting a dog from us, or did she just like shooting the breeze in our cafe? Was she actually trying to befriend me, or did she just need a listening ear?

Other customers were trickling into the dog petting area, so I stood to greet them. "Thanks for talking, Isabella," I said.

She glanced up from the dog, which she seemed smitten with. She struck me as a lonely woman who could really use a canine pet. "Of course. I've told absolutely all my friends about your fabulous place. We'll talk again soon, I'm sure!"

Bo walked in—capturing the attention of several females, including Isabella. He was wearing a gray sweater that played nicely against his red hair and beard. It also fit his muscles well, which was another attention-grabber for the ladies.

"Hey, sis, you have a minute?" He nodded at the customers in the room, and Isabella fluttered her eyelashes.

"Sure." Since the dogs were being quite calm, I opened the gate and met him near the coffee bar.

"Just wondering if you needed an extra hand in there? I noticed you were spending a lot of time with that blonde woman. Is she thinking of adopting a dog or something?"

I shrugged. "I honestly don't know. She just dropped in here and started talking to me. But it's okay—I shut the conversation down when other customers moseyed in." I glanced around at the nearby tables and no one appeared to be listening to us. "Actually, I wanted to talk with you, Bo. There's something going on up at that Ivy Hill Spiritual Center for Healing, I'm sure of it. I think someone there might've dognapped Coal."

"What?" Bo took my elbow and lightly steered me toward the back room, where we had to sidestep a couple of boxes of take-out cups. "What makes you think that? Wasn't that where someone was murdered?"

I might as well lay all my cards on the table for my big bro, who had always been my protector in grade school and beyond. I explained how Katie the masseuse had paid me a visit, trying to buy Coal, and how I suspected she'd wanted the metal tag I'd cut from his collar and hidden in my safe. I told him that Isabella knew Gerard, so it had been helpful to talk with her and get a better grip on Gerard's situation before he died.

I leaned against the sink. "I think someone's holding Coal at Ivy Hill. I heard a big dog barking last night when I visited the center."

"Wait—you visited the place?" Bo asked. "What'd you do, mosey in and ask if they'd seen your dog?"

"No, of course not. I'm not that dense—I didn't want to give my mission away."

Bo's eyebrows raised. "Your *mission?*"

"Yes, it's my mission to find my dog," I said huffily.

A small smile cracked Bo's lips. "Of course it is. I get it, sis, I do. But what if someone stole him to sell him? I mean, those

Danes can bring in a hefty price. Maybe they're trying to get him on the black market."

"Trust me, I thought of that." I shoved my wayward bangs out of my eyes. "I've scoured the internet, but there aren't any dogs fitting Coal's description or matching his photo for sale."

"Could be on the Dark Web," he said spookily.

"No, I refuse to believe that. It has something to do with that tag, I'm sure of it. I'll show it to you after work. It says 'Amber 457301.' Does that mean anything, you think?"

"Sounds like a girl's name," Bo said. "I'd have to give some thought as to what might use six digits like that."

"Well, think about it. Come to my place after work and we'll eat and figure out the plan. I'm signed up for a class at Ivy Hill tonight—not that awful drumming class I tried to do before. You could tag along and maybe one of us could snoop around?" I clasped my hands together. "Pretty please?"

Bo leaned against the metal shelving. "All right. I'll do it, but only for you, because I know what this dog means to you." His voice cracked a little, and he didn't have to say what we both knew—that besides him, Coal was all I had right now.

As I followed Bo out of the back room, I couldn't stop smiling. My big bro was on the case with me, and he would never let me down.

Bo FIXED a meal of chicken and dumplings that would've made Aunt Athaleen proud. I wished I'd spent more time in her kitchen, but instead I'd always migrated outdoors, exploring things with my dogs and daydreaming my life away.

As we ate, I caught Bo up on everything I'd heard, backing all the way up to Isabella's first conversation with her friend at Barks & Beans.

"I mean, it's possible the center director, Alice, is involved," I said, munching on a bite of salad. "Isabella said Alice and Gerard had some tiffs, and it sounds like their relationship was strained, but Isabella didn't think Alice would be stalking Gerard. Oh, yeah—and Isabella said Alice had some expensive rhino horn on her desk, so I guess she's doing okay for money."

My brother chewed his dumpling, waiting for me to wrap things up. In the silence, I felt an acute awareness that Coal wasn't pressed against my leg or sitting nearby, politely watching me eat. I hoped someone was feeding him well.

I tried to swallow my sadness and continued, my voice unsteady. "Oh, and unless I miss my guess, I think Isabella was having an affair with Gerard. She said she'd been over at his house for Christmas parties, but the way she lit up when she talked about the place, it was obvious she'd been there other times. Plus, she seems to be personally grieving about Gerard's death—she's even getting therapy sessions at Ivy Hill for it."

"I think I'm getting the picture," Bo said. "And you said you heard the dog barking upstairs at the center, right? How about this—we both attend the thriving class, then I'll slip out and check around upstairs. I'll be careful around that Doctor Schneider's office, in case he's counseling people."

"Sounds good." I took a sip of sweet tea. "Be careful, though. Gerard was obviously murdered, and the killer could easily be one of the employees at the center."

"Of course." Bo patted at his beltline, where I knew his handgun was securely holstered under his shirt.

"Just don't get too crazy with exercises if they're doing those, or someone might see that gun," I said.

"I might wear an ankle holster tonight," he said.

"We'll be ready for whatever," I said. "Now, let's go find my dog."

8

The Thrive at Life class met in the annexed part of Ivy Hill, so it could prove tricky for Bo to sneak back into the main section and check for Coal. The annex was connected by a greenhouse-style hallway that was chock full of warm-weather plants. I was particularly taken with an orange orchid that glowed like a flame of color in an otherwise green room.

We arrived in the classroom early because Bo arrived everywhere early. I think he felt it gave him an advantage over others, being the first to get the lay of the land and familiarize himself with a new setting.

A woman with short maroon hair and cat-eye glasses was arranging chairs in a circle. She wore dress pants and a blouse, so I figured that despite my yoga-pant garb, we wouldn't be doing exercise in this class. Bo jumped in to help the woman while I opened the door for an older couple who had just arrived. The couple had obviously been fighting with one another, since they were still scrapping around and didn't even thank me.

"Please, have seats in the circle," the maroon-haired woman

said. "I have handouts to give you once everyone arrives, but for now, I'll just introduce myself. I'm Alice Stevenson, the director of the center."

I struggled to hide my surprise. Here was one of my prime persons of interest in Gerard's death, which meant she could also be involved in Coal's dognapping.

After I sat down, Alice came over to shake my hand. "Welcome. And you are?"

"Macy Hatfield—that's my brother Bo who helped you with the chairs. We run the new Barks & Beans Cafe in town." I watched her face carefully to see if she'd recognize my name—which she would if she'd snuck into my house to steal my dog.

Her green eyes didn't flinch and her face remained placid. "How lovely to meet you! I've heard a lot about that cafe. Tell me, do you have éclairs? I'm a sucker for a homemade éclair."

I smiled. "I'm sure our baker, Charity, could add some to the menu. She's always on the lookout for new customer favorites."

"Please do! I'll have to drop by sometime. I'm not much of a dog person, but I think it's wonderful what you're doing for the shelter dogs." As more class members arrived, she darted a glance toward them, then looked back at me. "Please excuse me; I'd better introduce myself to the others."

As the perky Alice walked away in her eco-friendly shoes, I had to wonder if she'd dropped that dog comment on purpose, perhaps to throw me from guessing she might've stolen my dog. It seemed unlikely, given that it sounded like Alice and Gerard weren't tight, so he wouldn't have been likely to mention the metal tag on Coal's collar to her.

Still, I considered everyone in this place a suspect in Coal's dognapping until I could start ruling them out.

Bo settled in next to me on the chair I'd saved for him, which was closest to the door. "Find out anything?" he whispered.

"Not sure," I said. "Alice seems genuine enough—she said she doesn't like dogs."

Bo rubbed his beard. "Could be a smokescreen."

"I agree."

Conversation died down as Alice took her seat by the window. She clapped her hands together and smiled. "Welcome to the Thrive at Life class. This class is designed to help you work through personal wounds toward goals that will enrich your life. Together, we will help you forge new and healthy pathways to attaining your dreams."

Sounded like group therapy to me, and I wasn't too keen on the idea. I had no desire to rip into my personal wounds, especially in public.

"Let's begin with several deep breaths," Alice said.

Bo and I obediently breathed in and out on command, although I noticed the quarreling couple didn't make any effort to join in, since they were too busy shooting glares at each other. Had a marriage counselor referred them to this class? It seemed the only explanation given their apathetic attitudes.

There was only one other couple in the class, and the rest were singles. Most were older than us. I caught one woman watching my brother, probably wondering if we were an item, although our hair color was similar enough it was a dead giveaway that we were siblings.

"And now, let us close our eyes and contemplate for five minutes," Alice said, playing meditative music through a speaker connected to her phone.

As the bamboo flutes played, I nudged Bo. This would be the perfect time for him to escape. Without a noise, he got up, slipped between our chairs, and crept from the room.

Satisfied my brother had made his getaway, I relaxed into the tuneless music. My mind drifted to my South Carolina life, trudging to work with cliquish people who couldn't care less about me, renting a house I'd never truly liked, working through the fallout of an out-of-nowhere divorce...

Alice clapped and I jumped. "Miss Hatfield, did your brother leave us?"

I glanced at Bo's seat as if I'd just noticed his disappearance. "I guess so. He probably had to go to the bathroom," I said.

She gave me a doubtful look, like she expected me to elaborate.

It was time for a diversion. I scrambled to come up with something. "Uh...I was thinking, you said this class helps you cope with your deepest wounds?"

Alice gave a slow nod.

I sat forward in my seat and spoke clearly, so everyone could hear. "How would you suggest coping with wounds from a divorce?"

And thus I launched my alliance with over half the class. People shot me looks of solidarity and began raising their hands, offering up their own unsavory tales of their breakups. Alice was completely thwarted in her original plans for the session, inundated with wounds as deep as the Grand Canyon. I didn't know if she was a trained counselor, but she did make a decent effort to field questions.

Bo was all but forgotten by the time class wound to an end. Alice prescribed journaling homework for us and said she'd look forward to seeing everyone in a couple of nights. I wasn't sure I'd have any reason to show up—I was hoping Bo had located Coal and somehow whisked him into his truck.

Bo walked back into the room and started stacking chairs for Alice. She asked him where he'd been, and he said he'd gotten sick in the bathroom from what he thought was food poisoning. Bo had a natural gift for spinning the facts to his advantage. That's why it struck me as odd that he couldn't convince Tara he hadn't been unfaithful.

Alice seemed to believe his tall tale and told him he didn't need to continue helping her. He thanked her and walked back to me, so we left with no further ado.

I picked up my pace as we neared the now-vacated entryway. "So?" I asked.

He glanced around as we walked out the front door, then shook his head. The security guard or someone else must be lurking nearby.

Bo opened my truck door, which was an endearing habit of his and one Auntie A had worked very hard to instill. I climbed in, feeling chilly in my thin yoga pants. My heart deflated when I realized there was no Coal sitting in the extended cab seat, which is where Bo would've hidden him.

Tonight's mission had been a failure, then.

Bo got in and turned on the heat. "Sorry, sis. I guess you saw that I didn't have any luck. I didn't even hear a dog bark while I was in there."

I was glad it was dark, because a few tears slipped down my cheeks.

"But I did find something weird," he continued. "It had rolled over behind a statue in the upstairs hallway." He handed me something wrapped in a paper towel. "Isn't that a dog treat?"

I turned on the overhead light and gave the round pellet a sniff. "It surely is."

"So Alice says she doesn't like dogs—and dogs aren't allowed in Ivy Hill, are they?—yet there's a dog treat on the floor?"

It was nice to see my brother coming on board with my dognapping theory. "You're right. It seems suspicious."

"Also, I checked out Alice's office—don't give me that look. I didn't break in or anything. She'd left the door open while she taught her class."

"Did you find anything in there?"

He sighed. "Not really. I didn't even see that rhino horn you heard Isabella talking about. Alice seemed to have a lot of random knickknacks in her office. It wasn't like she'd invested a lot of money in her office decor."

"Yeah, Ivy Hill isn't exactly hopping. Maybe the golf course is more lucrative?"

Bo turned the heater fan down. "It's possible. Do you think Gerard was somehow embezzling from Ivy Hill, or even taking money on the side from lonely ladies?"

I cracked my window since the cab had warmed up too much. "Could be. Maybe that's why he got into it with Alice— she figured out what he'd been doing and called him on it." Rapping my nails on the door, I blurted, "I don't care so much about what Gerard was up to as I do about where Coal is. Do you think they're feeding him enough?"

"They'd be fools not to," Bo said quickly. "Like I said, he's worth a lot if they do decide to sell him."

I fell silent, hoping they didn't sell Coal before I could track him. It was a desperate situation, but I had no clue where to check next. It seemed like the only option left was to contact the police, but I couldn't prove Coal had been dognapped, much less by someone at Ivy Hill. I couldn't send the cops on a wild goose chase.

Bo pulled up to the sidewalk next to my place and led the way through the back garden. I was glad I had solar lights along the pathway, because I'd forgotten to leave the porch light on.

Bo had his house key ready and reached for the door. A split-second later, he shoved me off the porch and I nearly tumbled into a boxwood hedge. "Stay back," he commanded.

I hunkered down next to a solar light, wishing I could see what was going on.

"Someone must've broken in," Bo whispered, pushing the

door open with a loud creak. "Your door was cracked open and they've messed with the lock."

I shuddered to think of some stranger going through all my things. "Do you think they're still in there? We need to call the cops!"

Bo flicked on the interior light, illuminating the gun in his hands. "I'll clear the place," he said. I considered protesting, but if anyone could handle an intruder, Bo could.

I backed into the dark shadows in the corner of the garden. It seemed to take forever, but Bo finally came to retrieve me.

"No one's in there," he said. "But sis, you need to be prepared, because they went through a lot of stuff and it's messy. We're going to have to call the cops and have them dust the place before we clean up."

I felt like I'd been punched in the gut. Someone had been looking for Coal's metal tag, I was sure of it. They'd stolen him to find it, and when that effort returned void, they'd come back to my place.

I rushed into the house and headed straight for the hall closet, trying to block out the upside-down mess they'd left in my living room and kitchen. I pushed at the wall, shifted the panel, and retrieved my safe box, which appeared to be intact. I opened it, breathing a sigh of relief when I discovered the tag still safely tucked inside.

"So that's the tag that was on Coal?" Bo asked, peering over my shoulder. "Great hiding place. I'm so glad Auntie A had that specially designed all those years ago. You think that's what they were looking for?"

"I'm sure of it," I said. "I don't have many other valuables...just Auntie A's diamond ring, but that's in this box, too. Hang on and I'll check upstairs." I jogged up and checked my jewelry box and the spare closet. Although my drawers had been rifled through, all my jewelry was accounted for and

Auntie A's minks were still hanging in storage. My gun safe remained securely locked. "My valuables are still here," I shouted as I headed downstairs.

Bo was making another circuit of the downstairs. "Yeah, your TV is still in there, as well as your more expensive kitchen appliances, far as I can tell."

"The cafe!" I gasped, realizing the thieves could've broken into the connecting door. My arms started shaking. "Did they get in there?"

He looked at me closely and pulled me into a hug. "Don't worry. It looks like they didn't even try. Everything's intact in there. Now, come over to the couch and I'm going to make you a cup of tea."

I did what my brother said, wishing I could be more detached from this situation. But my things had been strewn around willy-nilly and they'd gone through my drawers. The intruder had access to all my things, from my toiletries to my old family photos. It seemed like they hadn't stolen anything, but it was impossible to be certain until I cleaned up.

Bo went into the kitchen and called the police while he put a kettle on to boil. By the time two police officers showed up on my doorstep, I was sipping on a mug of bracing cinnamon spice tea and had recovered a decent amount of my composure. An officer who was maybe in his early fifties introduced himself as Detective Charlie Hatcher, before waving at a younger man he introduced as Officer Butch Tomkins.

Bo and I walked them through the place, and I explained the home invaders might've been looking for the metal tag I'd found on Coal. I handed the tag over to the police, since I'd already transcribed it into Runic code on a piece of paper and tucked it back into the safe. I'd memorized Runic writing as a teen, when I was obsessed with all things Viking, and now I was glad I had.

While Officer Tomkins dusted for prints, Detective Hatcher questioned me about Coal's disappearance, as well as my movements of the evening. Given the intense look in his hazel eyes, I could tell he was taking this break-in seriously. He was a handsome man, with a dimple in his cheek that gave him a youthful vibe. Although he came across as an easygoing kind of fellow, something about the set of his chin told me he finished every job he started.

The officers finally wrapped up the scene and left, causing my buoyed-up emotions to sink like a stone. Bo insisted I stay at his house, and I was more than happy to agree.

"I'll install a deadbolt on this door tomorrow," he said. "And make sure you lock all your windows before you go anywhere."

"I *did* lock them all before I left. They broke in through the *door*." I was testy and I couldn't stop myself.

Knowing my propensity to get irritable when faced with situations I couldn't control, Bo promptly shut up. We walked up the darkened sidewalk and he let me into his house, which was a bungalow style place with a totally different flavor than Auntie A's oversized Colonial. Decorated with light colors and wicker furniture, Bo's house felt like it belonged on the beach instead of tucked into the Appalachian mountains.

"I'll sleep on the couch," Bo said. "You use my room."

Unable to formulate a coherent sentence, I nodded and trudged off to Bo's bedroom. I climbed into bed without changing, since I'd forgotten to bring my pajamas with me and I didn't want to raid my brother's closet.

Some stupid sliver of me longed for my ex-husband's embrace. Cheater that he was, Jake had always been highly affectionate—something that had drawn me to him. I tamped down my emotions, reminding myself of all Jake's vices, and went to sleep thinking of new ways to search for my dog.

9

THE TANTALIZING SMELLS of bacon and cooked peppers and onions woke me. I slid out of bed and pulled the comforter up to tuck it over the pillows, unsure if I'd be staying here again tonight.

As I walked across the hall to the bathroom, I was surprised to hear Bo's low voice in the kitchen. Was someone there? Maybe the cops had already figured out who had broken in?

I tiptoed down the hallway and peered through the open dining room into Bo's kitchen. He had painted his cabinets a beautiful shade of blue, which seemed to bring the ocean right inside.

He was holding a cell phone between his shoulder and chin. "You're being unreasonable."

Who was he talking to?

He set the phone on the counter, putting it on speaker before using a spatula to flip what appeared to be a veggie-laden omelet. "I know what it looked like, but you have to believe me, it was some kind of setup."

A woman's smooth voice filled the air, but her words were

laced with poison. "A setup? Why would some random employee try to set you up, Bo? Liv had *proof* you'd been having a fling with her. I've talked to her since you moved, and she's left me with no doubt you were lying to me."

I fought the urge to grab the phone and give her a 'what for'—Auntie A's term for the kind of verbal reprimand you wouldn't soon forget. The woman had to be Tara, and the fact that she believed Bo was untrustworthy proved to me just how little she really knew my honorable brother.

Even worse was watching Bo, who had blanched so much I could see his freckles standing out. He looked like he was going to be sick.

I backed toward the bathroom and dilly-dallied there for a few minutes. When I emerged, I whistled an off-key tune with all my might. I sauntered toward the kitchen, but there was no phone in sight as Bo slid the omelets onto plates.

"Hey, bro," I said, forcing a yawn so I'd look like I'd just woken up.

"I take it you overheard my conversation," he said, carrying the plates to the table.

"What conver—"

"You're a horrible actor, Macy. Yes, I was talking with Tara. Yes, she still hates me. That's about the size of it."

Bo grabbed two cups of coffee from the island and handed me one, then plopped onto a chair. "Have a seat," he said.

"Well...isn't it really early out there in California? I mean, maybe she wasn't fully awake yet."

"She gets up at four in the morning to work out," he said. "She's kind of an insomniac."

I savored my first bite of the golden, cheesy omelet. "Perfect," I said around my mouthful. "But honestly, she sounded like a real harpy or some other mythological demon-woman."

Instead of agreeing, Bo looked hurt. "She's really not. She's just reeling from this whole thing, that's all."

I couldn't understand why he was making excuses for her, but it really wasn't any of my business. I'd never gotten along with any of Bo's previous girlfriends, so why should I start now?

I took a giant swig of the bracing dark roast coffee, then glanced at my phone. The Lewisburg police department had called, but didn't leave a message. I hit the speaker button on my phone and called their number.

The receptionist put me in touch with Detective Hatcher, and he reported that they hadn't found any stray prints. "Whoever broke in used gloves," he said.

"Are you looking into what the metal tag could mean?" I asked.

"We're working on it."

"Are you going to do anything about my dog?" I'd given them a couple of missing dog flyers to put up near the station.

"Not much we can do that you haven't already done, Ma'am," he said. "But we'll be watching for him." He chuckled. "I mean, he's not the kind of dog you can miss, is he?"

I didn't find this fact amusing in the least, especially given that someone had been able to hide him for this long.

My heart started pounding and I took shallow breaths. "Just because he's a big dog doesn't mean he'll be a cinch to find."

Bo shook his head at me, obviously sensing I was about to lose my cool.

"Of course, Ma'am." The detective had gotten serious. "Like I said, we'll keep a sharp eye out for him. I'll update you if they find anything new with the prints, but in the meantime, be sure you get better locks on the door. The one you had was so old, it wasn't hard to jimmy open."

That much was apparent. As I hung up, Bo said, "I'll pick up a couple of locks at the hardware today and get them in for you by tonight. It's up to you if you're ready to stay there again —you know you're welcome to hang out here."

I couldn't allow myself to fall into my baby sister role indefinitely. "I might as well go home." An idea occurred to me. "Hey, do you think someone could cover for me with the dogs today? I'd like to get busy cleaning up my house. Summer only brought three dogs over yesterday, so I doubt it'll be a handful."

Bo was already standing to clear the plates. "Sure. I'll fill in for you, and Kylie was just saying she wanted to spend some time with the dogs. Although she's such a knockout barista, I won't position her over there for long—I need to keep her in the Beans section." He winked. "You take a break, sis. I'll bring the locks over and install them on lunch break. Do you have a weapon, just in case?"

Bo had given me my own .22 rifle when I turned sixteen, along with a hunter's safety course and numerous personal shooting trips to the range for practice. I'd kept it all these years, and I did practice with it occasionally, though not enough to make me a pro. Yet I felt reasonably confident with my home defense weapon.

"Still have the .22 in my gun safe," I said. "I'll be okay."

"Okay." He glanced at his watch. "I've got to book it to work. Call if you need anything."

As I brewed myself a fresh cup of coffee, I noticed a framed photo Bo had tucked behind a large Aloe plant on the windowsill. It was Bo and Tara, and they were both beaming on the beach. Tara's short, dark hair was windswept, and while her vivid green eyes were amused, they still managed to throw down a challenge. Tara was the kind of woman men never forgot.

Meanwhile, I wondered what men saw when they looked at me. My voluminous strawberry blonde hair resembled a fluffy mane unless I straightened it. My body was hardly sporty like Tara's—although I smugly recalled how my ex used to tell me I was curvy in all the right places. My eyes were a pale shade somewhere between blue and gray. Perhaps my unassuming appearance made me approachable, because everywhere I went, perfect strangers struck up conversations with me—just like Isabella had done yesterday.

I supposed my unwitting ability to draw people out was a kind of double-edged sword, as most abilities are. While it was often inconvenient, it also gave me deep blips of insight into worlds I might not have glimpsed otherwise. Like the teary old man at the optometrist's office who told me he was picking up his wife's glasses because he'd just moved her into a nursing home. Or the woman who was returning a toddler bed at the counter because she'd dropped out of drug rehab again and she couldn't bear for the foster parents to have the furniture she'd bought for her child.

Yes, people talked to me. I carefully repositioned Bo's photo on the granite sill. Perhaps there was a way to use my ability to gather information about Ivy Hill in a more direct manner. Taking classes hadn't worked—our stealthy recon missions hadn't turned up anything. What if I went closer to the source and talked with one of the employees, tried to get the inside scoop that way?

I wouldn't approach Katie directly—I didn't want her getting the wind up. Alice and Jedi already knew who I was, so it would seem strange if I showed up and started questioning them. But what about the Ivy Hill psychologist, Dr. Schneider? Isabella had nothing but praise for him, and although psychologists tended to be close-lipped, perhaps if I opened up about my divorce, I could inject a few questions about Ivy Hill without getting him suspicious. He had to have heard that dog barking the same night Isabella did, so I'd be interested to see how he explained that.

Fired up about my new plan, I finished tidying up Bo's place and locked up. The sidewalks had recently been swept, and red, pink, and white begonias had been planted along the streets. The town was gearing up for the Taste of our Towns event on the first of October.

Bo had managed to finagle a late reservation on a vendor table for Barks & Beans. Charity was working on pastry recipes she thought would sell well, and we planned to set up an espresso maker and a hot water dispenser, as well. It was my job to ask Summer about the possibility of having a couple of shelter dogs to pull in customers for the day, but I kept forgetting to talk to her about it.

There was no time like the present, especially since I was taking a day off, so I slid my phone from my pocket as I walked over to my house. I knew Bo had cut through my place on his way to work, just to make sure no one had tried to break in again. The door was securely locked when I stuck my key in, but my heart sank as I observed the mess the vandals had left behind.

I punched Summer's number, and she picked up on the fifth ring. "You busy today?" I asked.

"Yeah, but it's not for adoptions. We just checked in a litter of abandoned puppies. An entire *litter*. You don't want to know where they'd been dropped before a kind Samaritan brought them here. I've been giving flea baths all morning."

I was sure I didn't. "Actually, I needed to chat with you about the Taste of our Town event. We can talk later."

"Go ahead. I'm done bathing them, and the vet just walked in with their shots. My assistant can take it from here." She let out a huge sigh and I could visualize her propping her sandaled feet up on the counter.

"We were wondering if we could borrow a couple of shelter dogs for the event—nice dogs that wouldn't mind being kenneled and having people pet them throughout the day. We'll be in a covered tent and I'll keep them watered and walk them occasionally, of course."

Summer practically shouted into the phone. "Yes! What about taking a couple of these puppies for the day? That would be perfect! I'll bet someone would buy them."

It was a brilliant plan, actually. "That sounds great. Let's set it up. I'll let you go for now—"

"Why are you in such a hurry?" she asked with alarming astuteness. "Bo told me you were taking a day off, but he didn't say why. Is everything okay?"

I reluctantly told Summer about the break-in, assuring her that nothing had been stolen, but I had a lot to clean up.

"Why don't I come over and help you?" she asked.

I was surprised by the genuine concern in her voice. As I glanced around my overturned living room, I had to admit I could use an extra set of hands. "Don't they need you at work today?" I asked.

"Like I said, my assistant can handle things now. I did the most unpleasant work." She dropped her voice to a whisper. "And, to be honest, I could use a break. I'll be over in ten."

I hung up and started digging around under my sink for cleaning supplies. As the morning sunshine beamed through my windows, I felt a strange sense of elation, despite my recently burgled state.

It felt like Summer Adkins was becoming a friend, and I had precious few of those in my life.

10

Summer showed up at my doorstep exactly on time. When I opened the door, she had turned to gaze at my flowerbeds as if in awe.

"Wow. It must be great to have such established flowerbeds," she said. "I mean that rose—is it an heirloom variety? I haven't seen that shade before."

She pointed to a pale apricot colored climbing rose that covered a trellis. The cabbage shaped blooms were spectacular, and they smelled the way roses *should* smell.

"Yes, I think so. I keep forgetting to pick a bouquet for my table," I said. "They'll probably get frosted off in a couple weeks. Be sure to clip some for yourself before you go," I added.

Summer smiled like I'd offered her a bar of solid gold. "Sure!"

Once inside, Summer accepted a cup of coffee before we got down to work. It didn't take long until we were elbow-deep in cleaning, but many hands truly did make light work, and before I knew it, it was lunchtime.

"Bo will be coming over to install some locks for me soon," I said. "I'm not the chef in this family, but I can offer you a tuna or turkey sandwich, if you'd like one."

"Turkey sounds good," she said. "And I'm happy to fix it myself."

As I pulled the turkey from the fridge and arranged the bread and condiments on the counter, Summer asked if there'd been any news on Coal's whereabouts.

"No—actually, I was hoping you'd seen or heard something," I said. "The cops even know he's missing now."

"What about the previous owner's place? I mean, I know he's dead, but what if Coal broke out to try to run home?" she asked.

I'd had the same thought, but it would be quite the jaunt for a dog to run from our house into Fairlea, especially since there was quite a bit of through traffic on the road connecting us. Still, it was worth looking into.

"Maybe I'll drive over after lunch," I said. "Isabella told me what the owner's house looks like, so I think I could find it."

"Isabella...are you talking about Isabella Rhodes?" Summer's nose crinkled. "That hoity-toity rich bottle blonde?"

"I guess so," I said, though the woman hadn't struck me as hoity-toity when she let the shelter dogs sit on her lap at the cafe. "You've met her?"

"Oh, yes," Summer said. "She's been in the shelter before. She wears huge sunglasses and casual clothes, but I know it's her, all right."

I was confused. "You mean she's adopted pets there?"

"More like *returned* pets," Summer said. "She has this habit of picking up shelter pets like they're accessories, then returning them the first time they have an accident on her marble floors."

Shoot. I'd hoped Isabella would be a good customer, one

who could provide a good home to some of our Barks & Beans dogs. So much for that.

We sat at the table and started eating. Summer ripped into a bag of barbeque chips. "So, your brother...is he the one who likes to cook?"

I laughed. "Yes, because he took the time to learn how. Auntie A was more than happy to teach him, since I was such a hopeless case in the kitchen."

I found myself opening up about Aunt Athaleen and sharing how I'd landed back in her house. I'd just answered Summer's questions about Bo's years in the Marines when there was a knock on the interior connecting door and it began to open.

"That'll be Bo now," I said.

A tinge of pink crept into Summer's tan cheeks, and it dawned on me why she'd been steering the conversation toward my brother.

Summer had a thing for Bo.

Of course, so did a lot of women, but I had a feeling Summer didn't fall for just any dude. The way she stared at him—like he was the total package—told me that this girl got my brother in a way Miss Tara Fancy-Pants Rainey had not.

"Hey, bro," I sang out, a bit too loudly.

Bo clanked in with his tool belt and a couple of boxes of new locks. "Hey." He stopped and glanced at Summer. "Hi. What's up with that skittish Dalmatian mix you brought in today? We can't get that dog to calm down, so he's had to spend most of his time in our kennel area."

Summer wiped her mouth with a napkin. "Yeah, but he's beautiful, right? I figured someone might want that purebred look without paying for it."

"Purebred or not, he's a real toot," Bo said.

Summer laughed, and her face lit up. "Yeah, he definitely

is," she agreed. "Sorry about that. I can pick him up and take him back when I leave."

Bo shook his head. "No, we'll give him a little more time. Jimmy's found a chew toy he likes and maybe after a couple of walks, he'll settle down. I'll just drop him off after work, like usual."

I had noticed that Bo had recently commandeered my job of returning the dogs to the shelter. Maybe it was because he didn't want me using his truck, or *maybe* it was because he enjoyed seeing Summer. All the romantic wheels in my brain were whirring.

As Bo walked over and began drilling in the back door, Summer's eyes trailed after him. She unconsciously adjusted her ponytail.

Oh, yes. They might make an unlikely pair, but something told me Summer would make a much better sister-in-law than Tara ever could. She'd fit in here, for one thing. Also, she liked talking with me.

Let the matchmaking begin.

Once we finished eating, Summer and I completed the downstairs cleanup while Bo finished installing the locks. He made himself a sandwich before heading back to the cafe.

Summer got a call from the shelter and said she had to get back to work since one of the puppies wasn't eating. I thanked her profusely, planning to give her a substantial gift card to Barks & Beans in the morning.

I called Ivy Hill and asked to speak with Dr. Schneider. Once they put me through to the psychologist, I gave him a sob story about how I was feeling depressed from my divorce and I really needed to talk with someone as soon as possible. He said he was quite booked, but he could work me in for a thirty minute slot at eight tonight. I jumped on it.

In the meantime, I'd take a drive and find Gerard's place. I wondered if he had owned his house, and if so, who he'd left it to in his will.

Fairlea was smaller, population-wise, than Lewisburg, but more sprawled out. I passed the state fairgrounds and continued driving until I finally ran into Third Street, where Isabella had said Gerard lived. His house was unmistakable—bright yellow, with white gingerbread trim.

I cruised past it once, trying to get the lay of the land. No cars were parked in his driveway and a *For Sale* sign sat in the yard. The sign actually had the asking price marked on it, and it was unbelievably low for such a well-kept place. Either he hadn't left the house to anyone, or they wanted to unload it quickly.

When I drove around the second time, I parked along the street, right in front of Gerard's yard. If anyone asked why I was walking around, I could say I was interested in buying.

The yard itself was neatly kept, with a white picket fence surrounding the front porch and extending into the back yard. I walked around back, imagining Coal had been let out there to do his business. Just picturing my big dog lumbering around brought fresh tears to my eyes. It wasn't a surprise Coal had won my heart so quickly—unlike humans, dogs had no concept of faking their feelings. Either they liked you or they didn't, and Coal had immediately made it clear that he liked me.

Had Gerard loved Coal and been a good owner? He sounded like he'd been a good golf instructor, but that wasn't the same thing. What had he done to make Alice upset with him? And had Katie really been as close to him as she'd insinuated?

I found myself wandering up onto Gerard's front porch.

The mailbox was overflowing, and although I wasn't making an effort to snoop, my eye was drawn to a hand-addressed letter that bore a familiar return address—from Dylan Butler's art gallery, The Discerning Palette.

Did Gerard and Dylan know each other personally? Or was it just something like a generic invitation to an art gallery showing?

I'd left things in an awkward place with Dylan at the concert, when I'd told him about my useless broadcast journalism major. Maybe Bo could ask him over to the cafe on some pretense, and we could pick up where we'd abruptly left off.

The neighboring houses appeared to be empty, but I knew that was an illusion. Our county had a substantial number of retirees, and any number of them could be watching my every move. West Virginians were nothing if not suspicious of outsiders—I'd always figured it was the Scottish clan mentality. They wouldn't hesitate to turn me in or even to confront me. I backed behind a lush grapevine, trying to peer in the living room window.

Surprisingly, the furniture had already been removed and the house looked stark. No one had bothered to stage the place, then. Someone was looking for a hasty sale.

As I stepped from behind my leafy hideout, sure enough, a woman who appeared to be in her late sixties approached me.

"Were you looking at the house?" she asked, her dyed black hair harsh against her pale skin.

"I was, actually." Deciding to feign ignorance, I asked, "Do you know the owner?"

She frowned. "Oh, no, honey, he died. A young man, too. So sad."

"Oh, I'm sorry! What was it, an accident? Cancer?"

"You wouldn't believe it, but it was murder, they're saying."

She pressed a hand to her chest. "Not in this house, mind you. They found him on a golf course, bless him."

I tried to look adequately horrified. "And they put his house up for sale?"

The woman stepped closer. "They did, and not too long after. Are you interested? It's a lovely place inside."

"Oh, did you visit a lot? Were you close?"

She motioned to a blue Cape Cod a couple of houses down. "That's my place, just there. And Gerard and I were casual acquaintances, I'd say. He was friendly with his neighbors, but not obnoxiously friendly, if you know what I mean. Kind of kept to himself. He threw a street party at his place once, so that's how I came to see the interior."

"Did he have any pets? I don't care for pet smells in a house," I said.

She clapped a hand on my arm. "Oh, honey, he had the biggest dog you ever saw! A...what do you call 'em...a Great Dane, that's what. Law, but wasn't it a beauty, and a really polite dog, too. Didn't keep us up barking all night like some dogs do. I'm sure he kept the place clean, though. It didn't smell when I visited."

"What happened to the dog?" I probed, aware I was digging myself in deep if this woman ever caught me out and about with Coal in the future.

"I believe some of his coworkers came and took it. Must've gone to a new home, I reckon."

I had one more question I needed to ask, but I needed to figure out a plausible way to frame it. "I'm glad to hear the dog is safe and sound now. I've heard of some dogs running away from their new owners when they lose their first one so suddenly." Perhaps I shared a little of Bo's talent for spinning things.

She nodded, her attention wandering to the mailman, who had pulled up next to her house. "Yes, but that dog hasn't been around since, so I reckon it's doing okay. Nice talking with you. Be sure to call that number on the sign if you're interested." She marched straight across the front lawn toward her mailbox.

"Thank you!" I called out, heading toward my car.

Once inside, I leaned back into the headrest for a moment. Coal hadn't come back to Gerard's. And if he'd gotten hit on the road, people would've reported it because he had a collar and a dog like that was obviously someone's pet. No, in my mind there was only one possible explanation for his disappearance, and it started and ended with that crooked Ivy Hill center.

11

I WASN'T sure how Bo would feel about me traipsing up to the center again tonight, but I had an easy out because Bo sounded tired after he dropped the dogs at the shelter. He said he was going to order take-out and crash, but that I was welcome to stay over if I felt insecure at my place.

Strangely enough, I wasn't feeling as antsy as before, largely due to the locks Bo had installed. I told him I had soup at home and I'd be fine. I knew a large part of his exhaustion came from his thwarted early morning attempt to smooth things over with Tara. Bo never did anything halfway, and I knew he'd been all-in with his engagement to Tara.

Maybe if Doc Schneider was any good, I'd tell Bo about him. My brother needed to unpack some of the false guilt Tara seemed so willing to heap on his shoulders.

I pulled into Ivy Hill and was glad to see the battered police tape had finally been removed. It seemed slovenly to leave it up for so long, but maybe the police had instructed them to do so until the scene was completely cleared. I wondered how the police were doing with tracking down

Gerard's murderer. They hadn't seemed to be hanging around, but they'd probably completed all their initial interviews. Besides, they were probably concentrating their efforts on the golf course where Gerard spent most of his time.

Furious drumbeats echoed in the hallway as I stepped inside. Jedi must've left his classroom door wide open, perhaps in an attempt to spiritually heal everyone within earshot. I jogged upstairs, eager to escape the somewhat violent throbbing.

I rapped on Doc Schneider's door a bit too hard, and after a brief moment he opened it.

The doctor had long white hair, round glasses, and a bit of a paunch. Although he didn't have a beard, he seemed a jolly sort of fellow, kind of like Santa Claus. "Hello, hello. You must be Macy. What a lovely name. Come on in." He motioned me into his office, which was filled to the gills with indoor plants. He had the indoor waterfall going, no doubt to cushion against the racket of the drums below us. The overall effect was one of an oasis, and I guessed he had a hand in creating the greenhouse area downstairs.

I sat in a worn velvet chair, which instantly molded to my body and made me feel relaxed. I detected the faintest scent of something earthy, like the vetiver oil I used on my feet sometimes when I had trouble sleeping.

"Macy," he repeated, rolling the word on his tongue as if for good measure. "Is that a family name?"

"Yes. It was my grandma's name." Grandma Hatfield had urged my mom to reconsider naming me something so old-fashioned, but according to Auntie A, Mom wouldn't hear of changing it. After disliking my name all through high school, somewhere in my twenties I'd realized it fit me well, so I'd embraced it.

"Lovely," he said. "Now, Macy. You said you're in distress

about your recent divorce. How about you walk me through that experience?"

I gave a relatively short recount of Jake's numerous sins, but at some point the soft chair and the earthy smells and the waterfall combined into some kind of truth-telling trifecta for me, and I wound up delving further into my past.

I told the doc about my parents' deaths.

We had lived in a small house situated next to a creek from my birth until I was two years old. A freak flood occurred that November, sweeping away bridges and swelling rivers to unheard-of heights. This, in turn, flooded the creeks.

According to Bo, who was six when the flood hit in the middle of the night, Dad had carried us kids up to safety, tucking us in a cave on top of the hill before going back to get Mom, who had somehow gotten lost in the dark. Police later discovered that there must have been a rock-laden mudslide that plowed into the back of the house, which had pinned Mom to the ground. By the time Dad clambered back inside, the waters had risen so much, they were both trapped as the weakened house collapsed on top of them.

The sound of the waterfall seemed to have grown deafening as I once again imagined the watery grave my parents had to succumb to. "Would you mind turning that off?" I asked.

"Of course," the doctor said. His eyes were wide behind his glasses, but he managed to hold onto some level of equanimity. "This has obviously shaped who you are today. Now, you strike me as a very strong person, but perhaps it would be worthwhile to talk about this more." He glanced at his watch, and the room felt heavy with silence. The drummers had apparently gone home. I realized how vulnerable I was, sitting in a possibly empty building with a complete stranger. I wished I'd thought to bring the serrated pocket knife Bo had given me, just in case the doc wasn't so safe to be alone with.

I stood, anxious to leave, then realized I hadn't asked him anything about Coal. "Sure. Let's set up another appointment," I said. "Maybe next week?"

"Let me check my calendar." The doctor tapped at his tablet screen.

I continued, "It's so quiet, isn't it? You know, the other night when I came to a class here, I could've sworn there was a big dog barking upstairs."

The doctor didn't even look up or register surprise. "Yes— was that a couple nights ago? I heard it, too. I figured Jedi brought his dog to work again. He's not supposed to, but occasionally he does." He looked up from his screen. "How about Monday next week, same time?"

"I'll call back if that works for me," I said, unsure whether I could actually afford another session. I might wind up canceling—and I was strangely disappointed by that possibility.

I tried to shake the sinking realization that the dog treat and the barking could be explained by Jedi bringing his own dog to work that night. "So, what kind of dog does Jedi have?" I asked.

Doc Schneider stood. "A bigger dog...boxer, I believe?" He escorted me to the door.

I pried for information one last time. "My friend says the golfing is great here. I heard the last golf instructor was kind of rude...is there another one lined up yet?"

The doctor shook his head. "They've been interviewing, but no one's been hired. And the last golf instructor wasn't rude at all. Although I suppose he might have struck some people as abrasive. For example, his personality and our director's personality didn't seem to line up well. But he got along with most everyone else."

"Aren't personalities so interesting? I've been looking into

Myers-Briggs, but I don't think I've figured mine out yet. Was there anyone the golf instructor got on really well with?"

Now I was probably coming across as too nosy, but it was worth finding out if Gerard was particularly close to anyone other than Katie.

"He did tell me that he was interested in Katie Givens, our masseuse, but I didn't get the impression the feeling was mutual—"

A cheery voice sounded in the hallway. "Hello, Mark."

Katie was walking our way, in all her tan, tall glory. She wore a close-fitting workout outfit and looked like she'd been jogging...in the dark?

Had she been standing on the steps, listening in on our conversation?

She pointed at me. "Macy Hatfield, right? How's that big doggie doing?"

Was she putting me on? This must be a show for the doctor, as if she didn't know Coal had been dognapped.

I refused to play along. "He's gone," I said bluntly. "Someone stole him."

Katie's face shifted and she gave me a convincingly sympathetic look. "You're kidding me! When did this happen?"

"Actually, it was the same day you came over and tried to buy him from me." I smiled, feeling rather relentless. If she had my dog, I wanted him back. I couldn't outright accuse her, but I could dance around it with the kind of dagger-cloaked Southern politeness that let her know I was onto her.

"I'm pretty sure Gerard would've had him microchipped when he was a puppy." She gave a slow blink of her fake eyelashes. "He was an expensive dog."

I caught my breath, wishing I'd thought of that. Of course Coal would've been microchipped. I'd call the nearby veterinary clinics tomorrow and see if they knew how to find him.

I gave awkward waves to the doctor and Katie. "Sure. Thanks. Thanks to both of you." I knew I was muttering like a moron.

Katie swooped in on the doctor like she had her own issues to work through, so I hastily retreated down the stairs.

Once I got to my car, I rolled down the window for fresh air to clear my head. I hoped I hadn't come off as unhinged with Doc Schneider. I didn't need medication, I just needed time, at least when it came to getting over Jake. As for my parents, I would never finish grieving for them, but I'd learned to live with the fact they were gone long ago.

Far off in the distance, I heard a dog bark. I knew I was imagining things to think the bark sounded lonely. Now that I knew Jedi had a dog that frequented Ivy Hill (probably secretly, since Alice had said she didn't like canines), I had to admit that I might have been looking in the wrong direction for Coal. Especially given Katie's response when I told her he'd been dognapped—she had seemed genuinely surprised, even helpful, as she'd tried to encourage me about the microchip possibility. Maybe she was a great actress—after all, she'd been lying when she told me Gerard and she had been close—but somehow her surprise over his disappearance seemed legitimate.

I was back to square one with no idea as to who would've had a motive to steal Coal.

12

I woke early from restless dreams in which I'd found Coal locked in a dark cage while someone chased me with a golf club. Maybe my subconscious was confirming that the dognapping and the murder were connected.

I called Detective Hatcher to see if he had any updates, but he said there hadn't been any reported sightings of Coal. He sounded apologetic and not particularly hopeful. I figured he might be working Gerard's homicide, as well, which would obviously take precedence over my missing dog. I repressed my urge to ask him if there'd been any leads in Gerard's case and bid him a good morning.

I wasn't looking my best when I made my way to the cafe. I'd run a pick through my hair, which had only succeeded in making my pillow-induced cowlick stand up more. I was wearing the same jeans I'd worn yesterday and a plaid shirt that had shrunk in the wash, so I'd thrown a tank top under it that didn't quite match. Of course, Milo happened to be working the counter, and it was clear from his quirked lip and lingering stare that my appearance didn't really hit the mark today.

After traipsing into the dog petting room, I busied myself with straightening chew toys and re-organizing pet shampoo and other products on the shelves. Summer arrived with dogs in tow, and I only listened with half an ear as she elaborated on their canine idiosyncrasies.

"Macy." She shifted the leashes to one hand and walked over to me, placing her free hand on my shoulder. "You okay? You seem a little...spaced out?"

Yeah, I might *be* a little spacey. After all, my dog had been stolen, my house ransacked, and all my search efforts had been thwarted. Although I did have one possible lead on Coal, which I proceeded to follow up on.

"Summer, tell me about microchips. How do they work?"

"Animal microchips, you mean? Well, they're about the size of a grain of rice and they're usually injected between the shoulder blades of a pet. They can be scanned by animal control officers or shelters like ours to make sure strays don't already have a home."

"Did you notice if Coal was microchipped when he was brought in?"

"Yes, I think I scanned his."

My pulse throbbed in my hands. "So could we find him that way? You know, hunt down his microchip?"

Summer's deep brown eyes softened. "No, honey, we can't use it to track him. Now if someone picks him up and scans that chip, they'll know where to return him. But it's not like a homing device."

I sat down, dropping my face into my hands. I couldn't stand feeling so helpless.

"Here ya go, sis." Bo's voice filled the room and he handed me a warm mug. I wrapped my hands around it and savored the strong taste of our house blend, complete with extra cream and sugar.

I looked up, wiping at my eyes. Summer and Bo were both looking at me with such concern, I made an effort to pull myself together.

"It'll be okay," I said, wishing I could convince myself. "Summer, could you text me names and numbers of local vets? If I find the vet Gerard used, I'll have them list me as the contact person for Coal's microchip."

Summer nodded. "I'll be happy to." She passed the dog leashes to Bo. "I need to get back to the shelter. You think someone could make one of those?" She pointed at my drink and sniffed the air. "That's the best-smelling coffee I've *ever* smelled."

"Sure, I'll fix you one," Bo said, unleashing the dogs and ushering Summer through the dog gate.

I took another long, heartening sip of my brew, and as my senses started to wake up, I realized that Bo's tone of voice had changed when he'd offered to make Summer that coffee. But *how* exactly had it changed? I sifted through my memories of my brother, trying to slap a label on it.

Interested. That was the word. He was no longer feeling apathetic toward Summer, as he had before. He was showing interest in her.

I grinned as I took another swig of coffee. Bo did find Summer attractive, whether he'd admit it or not. Could the carefree ex-Mennonite pull my brother from his endless loop of regret over his muddled engagement?

I sure hoped she'd give it a try.

I was nearing the end of my work hours when Jedi sauntered into the cafe. I tossed a treat to my anxious schnauzer mix, walking him closer to the divider wall so I could covertly eavesdrop.

"Matcha tea, no sugar, local honey," Jedi said to Bo. His tone was snooty as he added, "I assume you *have* local honey?"

Bo clenched his jaw before answering. "Yes. Not only do I have local honey, it's ethically sourced with natural pollen and enzymes."

I had no idea what Bo was talking about, but apparently Jedi did, because he gave a smug nod and moved to the end of the counter to wait for his drink. I could just imagine Jedi telling Bo his energy was in the wrong place or that he was living on a lower plane today. I'd love to see how that played out. There was something about Jedi that I didn't trust.

And it only took a moment for me to realize that Jedi didn't care for me, either. Once he picked up his tea, he started walking toward the dog area...until he caught a glimpse of me. He turned and wheeled out of the cafe, sloshing green drips across the floor.

Bo shook his head and started murmuring to Charity, who'd brought fresh éclairs to restock the first batch that had sold out. I was glad she'd taken Alice's suggestion to heart and added them to the menu. It was clear from her response to Bo that she wasn't impressed with Jedi's attitude, either.

Why had I scared him off, I wondered? Had he felt guilty about something—like perhaps stealing my dog or raiding my house?

I leashed the jittery schnauzer and was about to take him out for a bathroom run when my phone rang. The voice on the other end was the last one I expected.

"Is this Macy? Hi, this is Katie Givens from over at Ivy Hill."

"Oh, yes. Hello?" I was at a loss for words.

She rushed on. "Listen, I found your dog."

My hands gave an involuntary tremble. As if sensing my weakness, the schnauzer gave a tremendous yank and pulled the leash from my hand. He raced directly to a man who'd entered the dog section, repeatedly jumping on the charcoal leg of his suit.

"No, down!" I hurried over to grab the leash, nearly dropping my phone in the process. "Sorry," I murmured to the man, who had backed up into a bench.

"Everything okay?" Katie asked.

I pulled the leash tight and sat down. "If you really found my dog, then yes, everything is great! Where is he?"

She lowered her voice. "I'm at work now. I'll explain when you get here, but you'd better come soon. Meet me in the Ivy Hill parking lot and I'll show you where he is. I'll be watching for you." She hung up abruptly.

My mind raced as I took the schnauzer out to relieve himself, hoping that would take some of the bounciness out of him. The entire thing could be a setup, from start to finish. Katie could've stolen Coal, searched him for the tag, then decided to unload him on me when she couldn't find it.

I wasn't stupid enough to meet her alone, even though it was the middle of the day. Besides, it would be easiest to transport Coal in Bo's truck.

The man in the suit had busied himself petting the other dogs, but he hesitantly asked if he could have a chance to pet the schnauzer, too. I led the frisky dog over to him and slowly took him off-leash. Raising on his hind legs, the schnauzer danced from side to side. To my surprise, the stodgy businessman cracked a smile and chuckled.

I was discovering that part of the fun of this job was watching customers pair up with dogs. People could surprise you with the characteristics they looked for in canine companions.

Jimmy arrived, ready to take over for me, so I briefed him on today's dogs. The burly man brought an unflappable sense of calm along with him, probably well-honed from his years of driving the high school bus. He was ecstatic when I told him the news that Coal had been located. "You get going, Miss Macy. I won't have any trouble holding down the fort here."

I gave him an appreciative smile and headed into the cafe. Bo put the finishing touches on a customer's coffee, then came around the counter to talk.

"What's up? You look excited."

I gave a little bounce of joy. "Someone found Coal!" I told him about Katie's call.

Without my asking, Bo volunteered to take me over in his truck. I felt a rush of appreciation for my brother. No matter what life threw at me, no matter how far apart we were, he'd always have my back.

If Katie happened to be lying and had designed some kind of trap for me, she was going to get a little surprise when I pulled up with my brother. She wasn't going to finagle her way out of this thing without telling me where Coal was.

13

WHEN I STEPPED out of the truck, Katie immediately came out to greet me. I grabbed Coal's leash and stuffed a few dog treats in my pocket as Katie began to explain.

"We have to walk out to the golf course," she said. "He's in a shed out there."

"How—"

"I don't know. I went down to meet the new golf instructor, Austin—Alice hired him a couple of days ago. I caught the sound of a dog barking near the woods, so I followed the noise to a storage shed. Your dog's in there."

She started walking toward the course and Bo fell into step alongside me. Katie didn't seem the least bit concerned at the sight of my brother, so it was possible she was actually telling the truth. Her long blonde hair flipped from side to side as she strode along.

"Austin hadn't heard the dog." She frowned. "But he doesn't hear anything, I think. He comes to work with his headphones in and leaves them in unless he's meeting with a client. I was lucky your dog was barking—he seemed worn out when I saw him. He's in a big plastic crate, although it looks like someone's been giving him food and water, and they must be walking him, since it didn't smell awful in there."

Or maybe he'd just been moved to the crate recently after being hidden somewhere else. I looked at Katie as she charged along in her dress pants. Had she taken Coal, hidden him at her house, then decided to put him in the shed and "reveal" him to me once she gave up on finding the metal tag?

I still couldn't rule that idea out.

When we reached the battered shed, Bo walked up to the door with Katie while I hung back. I tried to mentally prepare myself for the worst. Would Coal be traumatized? Emaciated? Would he even recognize me?

As they opened the door, a dog gave a weak bark. It sounded pitiful.

I stepped closer, trying to peer into the darkness of the shed. The dog's barks faded into half-hearted yelps. I finally caught sight of Coal's huge face when he smashed his nose against the metal door of his crate. With a gasp of relief, I stepped right up and stuck my hand out to him. He immediately began to lick at the door, trying to get to me.

My brother worked the spring latch and opened the door. The moment he was free, Coal didn't hesitate; he bounded straight out, inadvertently knocking me to the ground. He sat down on my stomach and started licking my face.

I gave him a long hug, then asked Bo to pull Coal off so I could struggle to my feet. Katie almost looked teary-eyed, but she'd already proven to be a good faker when she lied about her close relationship with Gerard, so I wasn't buying it.

"Thanks," I said, stepping into the cramped shed to get a better idea of where Coal had been kept. At least his abductor had put him in a crate big enough for him. Would it have been possible for a woman to drag such a huge crate out this far?

Maybe someone had helped her. Katie looked thin, but she was likely muscular, given her masseuse job.

The shed was stuffed with rusty yard maintenance tools and looked like it had sat untouched for years. I imagined most groundskeeping things had been moved closer to the newer golf course clubhouse for easy access.

"The door wasn't locked, was it?"

Katie shook her head. "Nope."

I stroked Coal's head, because he had basically glued himself to the side of my leg. "That doesn't really make sense—someone just stashed a huge dog out here, assuming no one would find out?"

Bo pulled the door shut and slid his phone from his jeans pocket. "I'm going to call Detective Hatcher and let him know we found Coal. They'll probably want to sweep this place for evidence, especially since it can't be a coincidence Gerard's dog was hidden at the same place he worked." He walked around the side of the building to talk.

"I agree." I put on a smile and turned to Katie. "Thank you so much for letting me know about him. You can't imagine how worried I was."

Katie still seemed genuinely happy about our reunion. "I'm sure! I hope you find whoever did this. I do need to get back for my next appointment, though." She gave Coal a smile and waved at me before jogging across the green. She had the nice, even strides of someone who jogged frequently.

Bo returned from his brief call. "The police will be coming over soon. They said we don't have to wait up for them, since Coal probably needs some TLC at home." He gestured to the dog, who had thrust his face under my palm and wouldn't budge.

"Yeah, let's go," I said. I didn't even have to pull on Coal's leash; he simply trailed along at my heels all the way to Bo's truck. I crawled into the extended cab seat and let Coal sit on the front floor. When we got back to my place, Coal got out and relieved himself before heading inside and curling into a ball under his blanket.

"I guess he's not hungry," I said. "Maybe that means they took care of him—well, aside from the fact that they locked him in a crate in a dark shed."

Bo patted my shoulder. "One thing's certain—he belongs here with you, sis. I can see he'd never try to escape from your house. Someone took him."

"Do you think it was someone he knew, and that's why he went with them?" I asked.

"Maybe, or they could've lured him out with a treat or something. Hard to say." Bo's phone buzzed with a text message and he glanced at it. "That's Charity asking if I can come over and verify a delivery. You going to be okay here?"

"Sure. I have locks on my doors and my dog's back safe and sound. Everything's peachy." I walked over and started filling my teakettle.

"So you'll lay off your Ivy Hill recon missions?" Bo asked.

I turned the water off and stared. "What do you mean?"

Bo grinned. "I know you went over there last night, too."

I huffed. "What, are you stalking me now? Can't a girl do things on her own around here? If you must know, I talked to the Ivy Hill psychologist about Jake."

Bo chuckled. "You don't have to explain. And no, I'm not stalking you, I just noticed you weren't home when I took my evening jog. I guessed you'd gone to Ivy Hill to search for Coal."

"You took a *jog* last night? I thought you were pooped!"

"I did, too, but I had a burst of stupid adrenaline." He placed a hand on the doorknob. "Tara texted when I got home."

I slammed the kettle down on the burner and cranked the

temperature to high. I didn't even have the words for Tara's hot and cold behavior toward Bo. Did she get her kicks out of running my brother through the emotional wringer?

"And? What did she say?" I demanded.

"She said Liv quit her job yesterday and walked out. Liv's the woman who accused me of seeing her while I was engaged."

"In other words, the woman who set you up." I poured hot water over a chocolate mint tea bag. "Want one?" I offered.

"No, thanks. I need to get back to work. Anyway, Tara started second-guessing everything about Liv when she quit so abruptly."

Second-guessing? She shouldn't have believed that liar the first time. I bit my tongue, taking a scalding sip of tea instead.

"I know," Bo said. "You think if she'd really loved me, she wouldn't have discounted what I said so quickly."

Yes, that was exactly what I was thinking. I poured myself a glass of cold water and took a drink to relieve the pain I'd inflicted on my tongue with the piping hot tea. I gave a stiff nod, since I didn't feel like vocalizing my rather strident opinions on Tara.

Bo seemed to pick up on my black thoughts. "Okay, well, I'll head on over. Call me if you need anything." He pulled my door shut.

I dumped more sugar in my tea before tiptoeing into the living room. When I pulled a blanket from the back of my couch, Coal snorted awake. He extracted his head from his blanket and gave me a mournful gaze before standing and lumbering over to the couch. I didn't even try to stop him as he situated himself on top of my cold feet.

As I clenched the warm mug between my hands, I tried to fend off the chill that was settling into my soul—toward Tara, toward Jake, and toward whoever had stolen Coal from me. I didn't want to turn into someone who saw nothing but evil in the world, but sometimes it seemed there were precious few truly altruistic people out there.

A text from Summer buzzed through. It said, *"You doing okay?"*

I'd completely forgotten to update her on Coal. I grabbed my phone from the couch and called her direct line because I knew she'd want to hear the good news. Come to think of it, maybe there *were* still a few caring people left on earth.

14

AFTER UPDATING Summer on the turn of events with Coal, which produced happy whoops and whistling on her end, I somehow drifted off into a nap.

My phone rang a couple of times, rousing me from a disjointed afternoon dream. I didn't like napping, mostly because it gave me just enough time to launch into a weird dream before I had to get up and do something else. I managed to extract my phone from under Coal's back, since he'd shifted positions and now sprawled along the end of the couch.

"Hello? Yes?" I said groggily.

"Hi, is this Macy?"

The male voice sounded familiar, but I couldn't place it.

"Yes, this is."

"It's Dylan Butler, from the art gallery in town." He paused. "This might seem a little awkward, but I felt we weren't able to finish our conversation the other night at the concert. I took the liberty of calling Bo, and he gave me your cell number. I hope you don't mind."

Well, this was interesting. I recalled the letter from Dylan's gallery that had been tucked into Gerard's mailbox. This was my chance to figure out if there had been any significance in that mailing.

I tried to show my enthusiasm. "Oh, sure. No problem. Glad to get caught up. What'd you want to talk about?"

"Actually," Dylan continued, "I was wondering if you'd like to go out with me. My friend owns a little restaurant that's really taking off. I'd love to spend some time with you."

Wow. I hadn't planned to plunge back into the dating scene so soon, although it had been months since my divorce.

"Sure, that'd be good." I stood to stretch and Coal shot me a baleful stare. It was clear he didn't want to be apart from me.

"Great—how about tonight, if that works for you?"

I stood stock-still, glancing around my living room as if it would give me a clue how to respond. Really, *tonight*?

Dylan spoke into my silence. "Of course, if that doesn't work, it's fine. I just knew my friend had a table open tonight and it's kind of hard to get reservations—"

I interrupted him before I could second-guess myself. "I'll do it." It came out sounding more like I was taking Dylan up on a dare than accepting a date with him.

"Sure, okay. I'll be by to pick you up around seven. I'm looking forward to it."

"Me, too," I said.

I hung up, promptly launching into full-on panic mode. Did I have one outfit that would be appropriate for a date? I had my DMV work separates, but they were bland and boring. Maybe if I threw a scarf on...but did people even wear scarves anymore? Mine were at least fifteen years old.

There was no time to go shopping, and I didn't know anyone I could borrow clothes from. Summer's style was a far cry from my own and besides, she was taller than I was. I looked up date night outfits on Pinterest, and all of them looked like something a "streetwalker" would wear (as Auntie A would say).

I reasoned that Dylan must've been attracted to me based on my normal dress style since he'd only seen me at the concert. I charged upstairs and plundered my closet, finally discovering a pair of dark jeans and a white blouse that I could spruce up with my camel sweater, jewelry, and a pair of suede low-heeled boots that were surprisingly comfortable. Coal followed me into my room, sitting outside the bathroom door as I showered. He plodded into the bathroom as I put on my makeup, unwilling to give me any space at all.

How was I going to leave my clingy dog alone in the house tonight? He was obviously feeling anxious, probably remembering that someone came in and snatched him the last time I left.

I called Bo to see if he could sit with Coal, and he was happy to help out. "You okay to go out with Dylan?" he asked. "I wasn't sure if you'd want me to give him your number."

"I'm fine with it. I mean, you worked with him a lot when you designed the cafe, right?"

"Yeah, he seems solid enough." He chuckled. "And I don't think he'd do anything questionable, since he knows I'm your brother."

That was probably an understatement. But then again, Jake had dared to cheat on me, brother or no brother. Granted, Jake knew Bo was across the country at the time.

I shoved thoughts of my ex behind me. "Okay, see you soon."

Bo came over early, as I'd expected, and I told him to help himself to whatever was in my fridge. He'd make a much better meal of it than I could.

Coal nuzzled against my hand a little, but I led him back to his pillow and told him to stay. I went ahead and walked out into the garden, hoping to clear my head before Dylan showed up.

I needed to stay focused, no matter how alluring Dylan smelled and looked. If he had any connection with Gerard Fontaine, I wanted to know what it was. It seemed like something the police might like to know, as well.

A polished black BMW pulled into an open spot on the street. Dylan stepped out, shoving his stylish sunglasses up on his head. He walked over to my garden gate and opened it for me.

"Thanks for going out so last-minute." His dark blue eyes played over my face. They stopped on my peach-glossed lips, like he was looking at some rare delicacy.

Was Dylan Butler a bit taken with me? It sure looked like it.

"No problem." I eased into the comfy passenger seat as he held the door open for me.

We didn't have to go far to get to the eclectic restaurant, which sat on top of a slight hill. As we walked in, a beautiful Indian mosaic and water feature added ambiance to the entryway, and the interior followed the Indian color theme with peacock blue, hot pink, and curry yellow shades throughout. Colorful glass lanterns hung from the fabric-draped ceiling and a fake fire glowed in an open fireplace, giving the booths an intimate feel.

"This is wonderful," I said. "So they serve Indian food? I do love a good curry."

"Yes, but my friend is also a deft hand with Asian cuisine," Dylan said. "And he just decided to add some French favorites to the menu, so it's really a fusion restaurant."

"Sounds amazing," I said. We situated ourselves and looked

over the impressive menu. I decided on the coconut chicken curry.

Dylan sipped at his chai tea. "So...we left off when you were telling me you'd gotten a broadcast journalism degree in college. How'd you get from there to running a dog cafe?"

His tone wasn't condescending—it was clear he was genuinely curious. I felt relaxed with him, like I could be myself. "I don't want to get into all the gloomy details, but I sort of burned out after college, at least emotionally. I didn't have the heart to hunt down a news reporting job back then."

"And what about the art history minor? Did you ever consider using that?"

I could see that Dylan was not only into the way I looked, but also into my art history mind. It was flattering that he was attracted to me, but I couldn't let that distract me from my objective tonight.

"I did. I actually worked at one of the art colony shops at the Greenbrier for a couple of summers, but then I felt the need to spread my wings and move to South Carolina." Which was where I'd met Jake the Snake.

"Ah! Was Julie the gallery director then? I'm good friends with her—she's the one who encouraged me to open my shop."

"No, it was a man named Gabe at that time." I bit into my curry and savored the explosion of flavor in my mouth. "But enough about me—what about your career? You say Julie helped you with your shop? I love the clever name of it, by the way."

"She did, and she helped me brainstorm the name. My parents also pitched in. They live in Fairlea."

There was my opening. "Fairlea—I think that's where Gerard Fontaine lived. You know, he was that golf instructor who was murdered recently. Can you believe that? A murder so close to home?"

I watched Dylan for any indication that he knew Gerard, but his face stayed neutral. "Oh, yes, I saw that—how awful. I wonder if the police figured out who killed him yet."

"I haven't seen anything in the news," I said. "Have you ever been to that Ivy Hill spiritual place where he worked?"

He took a sip of water. "A few times. I've talked with Alice, the center director, about paintings for the building." He grinned. "I can't say Alice has the best taste, but she's trying to learn."

"Bless her heart." I took a wild stab. "Are you the one who recommended she buy that rhinoceros horn?"

"Rhino horn? I've never seen that." He looked stymied. "Those horns would be way out of the price range she gave me for artwork. Maybe she got a knockoff?"

I supposed that was possible, although I wondered who in the world would spend time making knockoff rhino horns. Rolling on with my questions, I asked, "Did you ever golf there?"

"I have, just once. My dad has a membership, and one day last month his golf partner was sick, so I stepped in. Did a horrible job of it, I'm afraid. I met Gerard, actually, and he was none too kind about my rusty golf swing."

"I've heard he could be rude," I said.

"You knew him?" Dylan slouched back in the booth, but he couldn't conceal his tone of keen curiosity.

If I were feeling really candid, I might tell Dylan that I was now the owner of Gerard's Great Dane, but I didn't want to bring Coal to anyone's attention. "Not personally, but I've visited the place occasionally and I've overheard a few things."

Dylan leaned in toward me, unable to conceal his interest. "What things?"

"Oh, you know, that he was seeing the masseuse or that he

was getting too close with clients, that kind of thing." My eyes flickered from my curry to Dylan's face. "All lies, I figure."

Dylan looked pensive. "Yeah, but sometimes, where there's smoke, there's fire."

"Very true."

We moved on from the subject of Gerard, passing the rest of the date trying to figure out if we had any of the same interests, aside from art and music. It seemed we couldn't be more different. He liked cats; I liked dogs. He was an entrepreneur and a leader; I was most comfortable being a follower. He enjoyed staying inside; I loved puttering in the flowerbeds.

But by the end of our date, I had to admit I'd enjoyed spending time with Dylan. When he asked me to a showing at his gallery in a couple of weeks, I hesitated, knowing I was still in a vulnerable place emotionally.

"I think it'll be okay, but I'll call and let you know for sure before then," I said as he walked me to my door.

He smiled as we stood on the doorstep, but didn't attempt to lean in for a kiss, which I appreciated. At my knock, Bo unlocked the door from inside and flipped on the porch light. I heard Coal's gigantic paws pounding toward the door.

After thanking Dylan again for the lovely meal, I went inside, where Coal sat directly in my way until I caved and gave him a thorough petting. My cheeks felt a little flushed, but Bo was watching his favorite show, so he didn't notice.

"Have a good time?" He didn't turn around.

"I did. There's a great new restaurant in town you need to visit. I brought you some of my leftover chicken curry." I spotted his keyring on the counter and set the takeout box beside it so he wouldn't forget.

"Thanks." He paused his show and glanced at me, but thankfully my blush had toned down. "I'll head on home. Coal did okay without you, although he did steal my spot on the couch and I literally couldn't budge him for half an hour."

As if sensing he was being ill spoken of, Coal leaned against my leg so hard he almost knocked me over. "Come on, you couch-stealing doggie," I said, rubbing behind his always-alert ears. "I'll take him up and change to my PJs. Thanks for coming over, bro."

Bo jumped to his feet, flipping the TV off. "I'm glad your dog is recovering from his ordeal. Oh—Detective Hatcher called and said they checked out the shed at Ivy Hill, but didn't find any trace of who could've taken Coal." He grabbed his jacket from the back of the couch, shrugged into it, then scooped up his keys and the box of leftover curry.

I sighed. "Of course they didn't." The person who'd stolen Coal had been smart and careful—the exact kind of person who'd also make an effective murderer.

LATER, I snuggled under the quilts on my bed with a mug of hot chocolate and a psychological thriller. After reading over the same paragraph four times, I had to admit I couldn't focus. Something was niggling at the back of my mind.

Dylan had quipped that where there was smoke, there was often fire. What kind of fire—or fires—had Gerard been involved in? Doctor Schneider had categorically denied that Gerard was seeing Katie, even though Katie had made it sound like they were close. I was fairly sure that Isabella and Gerard had some kind of romantic involvement, but I wasn't a hundred percent certain.

I stroked Coal's face. "I wish you could talk to me, old boy. What was Gerard like? Was he even nice to you?"

Coal whined and licked my hand. He let out a groan, then

slumped over to his pillow and pawed at it before settling down to sleep.

I supposed it didn't matter how much Gerard had loved Coal, because now he was happy with me. And I'd love my big lug of a dog the rest of his days.

15

WHEN I HEADED over to the cafe the next morning, I found Bo unloading a new shipment of coffee beans in the back room. "This stuff is from my friend in Costa Rica. They're some of the best beans on the planet, and I'll be using them for Taste of our Towns tomorrow," he said. "How about I make us a cup so we can do a little quality control?"

"Sure, that sounds great," I said, ambling over to the doggie section. Summer would be along any minute to drop off our dogs of the day. She'd mentioned bringing a couple of the stray puppies over so we could socialize them a little before we set up for the outdoor event tomorrow.

When Summer strode into the cafe, I had to control my gasp. She was wearing a sleek black motorcycle jacket and trim black pants with brown wedge boots. Her hair was a different color—perhaps her *natural* color? It was a dark honey blonde that was absolutely striking with her coffee brown eyes. She'd pulled it all back into a sleek, braided updo, and her natural makeup accented her glowing skin.

In short, she looked just as glam as Isabella or any of those other socialites in town.

Milo, who happened to arrive at the same time, let out a slow whistle as he edged around Summer, who was wrangling two frisky puppies on leashes. "Not to objectify you, Summer, but you look *so* one hundred in that outfit today. And your hair!"

I shot him a look. "You are objectifying her, Milo. Get back to work."

Summer laughed. "I don't mind. It's nice to know DeeDee got this hair color right. I wanted to go back to my natural shade, but it's quite the process when you're starting with purple."

Bo emerged from the back room, bearing a bag of his precious Costa Rican beans. He glanced at Summer, then did a double take.

"Summer!" He fell silent, clearly searching for words. "You look nice."

Nice? That was the best my brother could do?

"Thanks," Summer murmured before hurrying into the dog area, nearly tripping on her active canine cargo.

I took the leashes and walked the puppies, which were adorable. Their faces and coloring looked like shelties, but their fur was shorter.

"Your hair looks fantastic," I said to Summer, not looking directly at her since she was obviously embarrassed. I wondered why she'd dressed up, but something told me it was a capricious idea to impress Bo.

Bo walked over with a couple of coffees. He handed one to Summer, looking right at her as he did so.

She directly returned his gaze. Silent fireworks were going off, I was sure of it.

"Thanks," she said, a smile curving her lips.

Bo smiled back. "Sure." He handed me the other coffee, then walked back to the cafe.

Summer gave a tiny sigh before launching into a rundown on the puppies. She'd only brought the two pups, so I could work with them before Taste of our Towns tomorrow.

"This litter is going fairly quickly, but we still have two left at the shelter," she said. "They look pretty much like this sister and brother, but they're both boys and they're...well, let's just say *rowdier*."

"Gotcha," I said. "Thanks for bringing the calmer ones." At this opportune juncture, one puppy—I was pretty sure it was the sister—pounced on my shoe like it was a hostile attacker and began to chew the end of it. I picked her up and moved her to the mat overflowing with chew toys.

"High energy dogs." Summer sipped at her coffee, which had finally cooled off. "Wow, this stuff is the bomb."

"I know. You'll have to tell Bo that," I said coyly.

"I sure will." She gave the puppies final pets, apparently not catching the romantic intent of my comment. "Have a great day, Macy."

As she walked back and struck up a quiet conversation with Bo, who happened to be lurking at a table nearby, I smiled to myself. There was hope on the horizon for my brother, if only he'd give up whatever falsely placed loyalty he still felt toward Tara.

AFTER TAKING a lunch break at my place with Coal, who frolicked happily like he'd reverted to his puppy years, I headed back to the cafe. Glancing around at the packed tables, I realized that Barks & Beans was actually succeeding in every way we had dreamed it would. Soon, we might have to hire more employees. Aunt Athaleen would've been so thrilled that her house was the conduit for our income, and that we were both settled back in our wild and wonderful West Virginia hometown.

The door opened and Isabella's older friend, Mary Anne, walked in. She looked impossibly stylish—I couldn't imagine she was dropping in to pet the dogs in her custom-tailored pants ensemble.

Two tween children were keeping the puppies busy, so I was able to inch closer to the cafe. Mary Anne gripped her coffee mug with bejeweled fingers and sat at a nearby table. I sank back into my chair, trying to look preoccupied with dog business.

A dapper older man walked in and waved at her and she absolutely lit up. Were they married? *Could* people gaze at each other so longingly after years of matrimony? I felt ill-informed on the inner workings of healthy marriages.

Auntie A's husband, Clive, had died in his early fifties, leaving her with a huge house, no children, and nothing really good to say about the man she'd married. I'd never had the impression she missed him much.

Obviously, our parents had loved each other—after all, Dad lost his life trying to save Mom—but I had no memories of their day-to-day interactions.

The man walked over and joined Mary Anne at her table. She took his hand and they began to murmur together. They were both wearing wedding bands, so it would appear they were indeed married.

The puppies started chasing each other around the doggie area, so I turned to check how things were going. Sure enough, the tweens were egging the pups on in their roughhousing.

I intervened, largely because I couldn't hear Mary Anne's

conversation, but also because the entire room felt chaotic. "Let's try to keep it down a little, y'all."

The kids gave me embarrassed grins and settled onto the floor with puppy toys. I tuned back in to Mary Anne's conversation, since her table was within earshot.

"We should go," she was saying. "Oyster roasts are in vogue —Isabella's told me about them. She went to a couple when she visited Savannah last spring."

The man chuckled. "They're going to truck fresh oysters all the way into our mountains?"

Mary Anne gave an earnest nod, oblivious to her husband's ribbing. "Oh, yes. They do bring some shipments to the Greenbrier, so why not to Ivy Hill?"

All my senses perked up at the mention of Ivy Hill, as if I'd bolted down a cup of espresso. I really needed to stop paying attention to that place, but I was still convinced someone who worked there had stolen Coal.

"Everyone we know has been invited, love. I think you'll want to tour their golf course—it's cheaper than the Greenbrier, but I've heard it's nearly as nice. I'd just need to call and RSVP, since it's tonight at seven. What do you say?" She gave a hesitant smile that seemed to say, *If you love me at all, you'll go along with this.*

I could tell the older man was putty in his wife's hands. He set down his mug and clasped her other hand. "Of course, darling. Whatever you want. An oyster roast will be a unique experience, I'm sure."

Mary Anne started talking, mostly to herself, about clothing options for the oyster roast. My attention drifted back to the puppies.

Should I book a reservation for the event and take Bo along? I could give it a final poke-around for clues as to who took Coal and how they were connected with Gerard's death.

The tweens' parents called them back into the cafe. I commandeered the puppies' leashes, threw on my jacket, and took them for a walk. The lively pups hadn't had a decent nap all day. If anyone showed interest in adopting them tomorrow, I was going to feel obligated to tell them these were high-energy dogs.

My phone buzzed with a text. The puppies strained at their leashes, but I stood transfixed by the strange message. It said, *"Come to the oyster roast at Ivy Hill tonight. I have information regarding your dog."*

I tried to look up the name that connected with the number, but my internet search yielded nothing. The person was being cagey.

"Who is this?" I texted back.

The response was fast. *"I'm the one Gerard trusted with his dog."*

Was the person insinuating that Coal should have gone to them? The puppies shuffled around my feet, nearly tripping me, so I led them through the side door.

My phone buzzed with another text. *"Come alone and meet me in the attic at eight."*

The mystery person had to be joking. No way I was going to waltz into a meet-up with someone I'd never even met for some kind of vague information about Coal. He'd already been rescued from his dognapper—but maybe this person didn't know that.

"What kind of information do you have?" I texted, sensing a setup.

It took a few minutes for a response. I had just started refilling the puppies' water bowls when my phone buzzed. *"I think I know why someone took your dog. I wanted to talk with you before going to the police."*

My mind raced to the metal tag I'd suspected the

dognapper had wanted. Did this person know about that? The fact that they planned to go to the police seemed to indicate they were on the up and up.

"Why do we have to meet in the attic? Why not in the open?" I texted.

"Because I'm an employee at Ivy Hill. I don't want to jeopardize my job."

That made sense. I doubted any of the Ivy Hill employees would try to attack me on the grounds with such a crowd outside. And although I didn't trust Katie, she didn't seem the type to go in for all this subterfuge. If she'd wanted to share information on Coal, presumably she would've done so when she'd led me to him.

"I'll be there," I finally texted.

"Straight down the hall, last door in the middle."

I looked up the phone number for Ivy Hill and made one reservation for the oyster roast. Although I was tempted to ask Bo along, the mystery person had said to come alone. I could look out for myself without my big brother hovering around, couldn't I? Besides, I'd take my pocket knife and keep my phone handy in the attic.

Hopefully, I'd unwrap the mystery behind Coal's hidden metal tag.

16

THE WOMAN I'd made my reservation with had mentioned several times that I should wear something "warm and casual" to the oyster roast, so I layered my short sleeve shirt with a blazer, then grabbed a jacket, just to be on the safe side. It had been a warm September, and evenings hadn't been too chilly yet, but a weather front was moving through and promised cooler temperatures overnight.

Perceiving I was going to abandon him for a stretch of time, Coal swirled around me as if corralling me. His tail was working overtime, and every time it bopped into my leg, I wondered if I might actually get a bruise.

"I won't be gone long," I assured him. I hoped that was the truth, because I didn't want to be alone with the texter for any extended period. How had this person gotten my cell number, anyway?

As I tucked my knife into my pocket, Bo called from his house. He must've already returned the puppies to the shelter.

With no preamble, he said, "They peed all over the truck. Why didn't I think to put them in the crate before I left?"

I tried to sound relaxed, although I was in a hurry to get out the door. "Sorry. I should've warned you they're little live wires."

"I'll say. You sure you can keep a handle on them tomorrow at Taste of our Towns? The streets are always packed, and I don't want them breaking loose."

"They'll be in the kennel, so it's not like they'll be running free. I'll handle all their potty breaks, food, and toys, so all you'll need to do is get that metal kennel out of Auntie A's shed and haul that over to our booth. I plan to get there at six, so I can set up the dog stuff while you help the others get the food and hot drink area ready. Sound good?"

"Sounds good." He was rustling around his kitchen; I heard the fridge door slam and the clang of a pot.

"I'll let you go, bro. Sounds like you're getting supper ready."

"Charity gave me her beef stew recipe, and it uses maple syrup. I can't wait to try it out. You want me to bring some over later?"

I glanced at Coal, who had given up on corralling me in favor of stretching out full-length next to my back door, completely blocking it. "Uh, no. I'm going to hang out with Coal and watch some old movies." It wasn't a *total* lie, because I fully planned to hang out with Coal later on and watch movies. I just needed to meet up with some unknown informant at Ivy Hill first.

After saying goodbye to my brother, I did a final check of my appearance in the hall mirror. Apparently, my hair had absorbed all the humidity in my house, leaving its waves fluffed beyond all control. I couldn't wait until fall arrived to dry the mountains out—and my hair.

I pulled it back into a loose bun and stared at Coal, who met my look with an angelic gaze. "You're going to have to get out of my way," I said, not falling for his mask of innocence.

He tried to talk back with a whining growl, but I told him to knock it off and shooed him toward the living room. "I have to do this one thing," I said. "Just *one* thing, then I'll be back before you know it."

I'd heard of people leaving their TVs on so their dogs didn't feel alone, so I figured I'd give it a try. After all, Coal was going to *have* to stay by himself sooner or later—my brother couldn't dogsit all the time. I pulled up the old movie channel and *Rear Window* was showing, so I turned it down in case the commercials got loud. Setting the remote on the counter, I grabbed a pile of Barks & Beans business cards. I figured I might as well take advantage of the opportunity and hand them out at the party. I zipped out the door before Coal could careen back toward me.

Feeling more than a little guilty for lying to Bo and leaving my bereft dog on his own, I hurried to my Honda and whisked away. An oyster roast would be fun, I reasoned. I could schmooze with the locals, hand out business cards and try an oyster or two, then sneak upstairs for the rendezvous with the informant.

The long drive was lit with luminarias that gave a party feel, and a long tent protected tables in the front yard. The tent was draped with hanging strings of lights, and sunflower arrangements had been placed at each table. Ivy Hill had spared no expense when it came to throwing this oyster roast, and I wondered what the motivation was for such a snazzy soiree.

Alice stood by the food table, demonstrating how to use the small knife to shuck oysters. She seemed quite familiar with the process, so I imagined she'd been the one to organize this event.

She caught sight of me and flagged me down. "Macy Hatfield! I saw your name on the guest list, and I'm so glad you decided to come. I was a little unsure if you were happy with your Ivy Hill experience, given that you never returned to my class."

Apparently, Jedi hadn't reported that I'd cut and run on his class, either. That made sense—he wanted to look good for his boss.

"I'm sorry. Yes, my brother and I enjoyed it, but I just needed more one-on-one attention." I grabbed a sturdy paper plate and moved toward the food line, hoping Alice would take the hint and leave me alone.

She didn't. Instead, she got closer and gave me an expectant look. "But you came tonight, so I'm hoping you want to throw your support behind Ivy Hill?"

Our support? Like a bolt, I realized she was talking about Barks & Beans, not about Bo and me individually.

"Oh, yes. We're happy to support your center." I was being overemphatic, but we certainly didn't plan to blacklist Ivy Hill to any of our customers. Unless, of course, my informant gave me some solid accusations against the center tonight. "In fact," I continued, pulling my cards out of my pocket, "I brought some of our business cards, if you wouldn't mind sharing? I'm sure our customer bases overlap quite a bit."

Alice seemed appeased as she reached for the cards. "Of course! We'd be delighted. I'll place these on the sign-in table. Thanks so much for coming, Macy."

I turned back to the food table, which was laden with mesquite shrimp, beef kabobs, and all sorts of beautiful side dishes. Servers manned an open-fire grill off to the side of the tent. The roasted oysters were shuttled to the end of the long table, where guests kept busy pulling the meat from the shells.

A man spoke close to my ear. "Think anyone will find a pearl?"

I knew that voice. I turned to face him.

"Dylan!" I was happy to see he'd shown up. "Actually, I've

heard it's rare to find pearls in oysters."

The man was dressed exactly how you'd imagine an art gallery owner to appear. His dark corduroy jacket looked equal parts expensive and relaxed, and his unbuttoned denim shirt played well against his ink blue eyes.

There was chemistry between us, all right. At least on my side of the equation.

"I figured it would be interesting," he said, glancing around. "These guests are the type of people who might frequent art galleries. He reached into an interior jacket pocket and produced his own flyers for his gallery. "I thought I could mill around, get the word out on The Discerning Palette, you know?"

I gestured to the pile of Barks & Beans cards Alice had positioned neatly on the sign-in table. "I had the same thought," I said.

Dylan chuckled. "We're a couple of marketing mercenaries, aren't we?"

I grinned and glanced down at my plate. Dylan took the hint. "You go eat," he said. "Your food will get cold. Let me know how the oyster is."

I nodded and found a table while Dylan spoke with a couple of the guests. As I bit into the tender beef, I scanned the party guests. Isabella had just arrived, hanging on the arm of a man who looked to be twice her age. She wore a large hat and shades that would fit in perfectly at a polo match. Isabella's friend Mary Anne was seated at a table with her doting husband.

The wealthy residents of Lewisburg seemed to have turned out *en masse*, which was likely the outcome Alice had been shooting for.

All the employees I'd met were also in attendance, and I wondered which of them was my mystery texter. Katie looked tan and svelte in a pink sheath dress, although I imagined her exposed legs were going to get cold as the evening wore on. Jedi hung around the outskirts of the crowd, wearing suit pants that were too large on him and a wrinkled dress shirt. Doc Schneider was working his way through a heap of oysters. A pretty older woman sat by his side, and I assumed she was his wife.

A younger man wearing cargo pants and a golf shirt made his way to the food table. Noting the headphones tucked around his collar, I realized this must be the new golf instructor, Austin. Given the way he ignored the guests, I had a feeling he wasn't going to last long in his job.

Alice picked up a glass and dinged on it with her fork. "Your attention, please! Thank you so much for attending our first oyster roast at Ivy Hill. Thanks to generous donors like you, we are able to continue to provide programs and outlets for the Lewisburg community. Please take a moment to sign our guest book and share your email with us, if you want to stay up to date on upcoming opportunities." She gave an enigmatic smile. "We're very excited about some recent developments, and we can't wait to share our news with you via email, once we get the go-ahead. Thank you for your support!"

The crowd began to dissipate after Alice's speech, with latecomers settling in at tables the early diners had started to abandon. I stood, found a trash can, and dumped my plate. I glanced around for Dylan, but didn't see him.

Checking my phone clock, I realized it was already a quarter to eight. I was fairly certain guests were allowed to ramble around the grounds, so I confidently walked toward the main building. Sure enough, the battery candles and twinkle lights were on. Voices approached in the downstairs hallway, so I dodged upstairs and took a breather on the landing.

Only one door in the wide hallway stood open—the door to

Alice's office. A lamp on her desk was flipped on, and I stepped closer to peek inside. The decorations were strange, for sure, but I didn't see any rhino horn. Maybe Isabella simply made that story up to impress Mary Anne. The desk lamp was the only pretty thing that caught my eye. I'd always been a fan of dragonflies, and the green stained glass lampshade featured several large dragonflies, their wings overlapping. Why had Alice left her door open with so many strangers around?

I had to admit that Alice could be my mystery informant, but if so, why would she give me information before sharing it with the police, when she was the director at Ivy Hill?

Stepping away from her office, I fingered the knife in my pocket. Thanks to regular practice with it, I could pull it out and flip it open in one smooth movement. It seemed unlikely I'd need it for this covert meeting—after all, the informant had seemed anxious to tell me something. I doubted it was a setup, because I wasn't a threat to anyone. I had no more clue who had killed Gerard or stolen my dog than any of the townspeople around here.

Riding on my temporary wave of confidence, I walked straight to the last hallway door and opened it. It gave a resounding squeak on its hinges. I cringed, knowing I'd lost any element of surprise. A set of stairs led, presumably, to an attic. I didn't bother to soften my footsteps as I pounded up to see who awaited me.

I topped the landing and peered into the darkened room. I couldn't see anyone—maybe I'd arrived too early? I was fumbling for my phone to turn on my flashlight when I heard someone pull on a chain. A light bulb flickered on at the opposite end of the attic.

A man sat in a rocking chair, waiting for me. And he was the last person I'd expected.

Doctor Mark Schneider.

17

I STARED at the doctor and he stared at me.

Finally, I worked up the nerve to say something, although it was completely inane. "So, you sent me that text?"

He nodded, motioning to a cracked leather seat across from him. "Please, have a seat, Macy."

As I walked over, he continued to explain. "I apologize for all the subterfuge, but I didn't want anyone here knowing I was connected with you in any way. It's safer for you."

I sat down, bits of dried-out leather sprinkling my pants. "Why? What do you mean? And what kind of information do you have on my dog?"

The psychologist adjusted his glasses. "Let's start at the beginning, shall we?"

I nodded mutely, anxious to get to the reason for this clandestine meeting.

"Gerard talked to me more than I let on to you," he said. "Not as a psychologist, mind you. More like...someone he could trust. I wouldn't say we were close friends or anything like that. Yet he directly approached me the week before he died."

I leaned forward. "And he told you something about his dog?"

"Yes. He told me if something happened to him, I was to immediately take his dog to a shelter, and that I couldn't give the dog to anyone at Ivy Hill. It was clear he thought someone was out to harm him, and I asked him who he was afraid of. He wouldn't elaborate more than to say he feared for his life due to something he was transporting for someone else."

"Someone at Ivy Hill?"

He shrugged. "That's what I assumed. Of course, I tried to get to the root of his fear, but he wouldn't tell me anything. I got the impression his dog was valuable in some way, more so than a normal dog, but he never confirmed that idea."

"So when Gerard was killed, you realized he had good reason to fear," I said.

"Yes. The moment the news broke, I grabbed the house key Gerard had made for me and went to his place. I had to look around a little, but I found the dog registration papers he'd placed on his desk, just in case. Then I managed to load up his dog." He chuckled. "No easy task, that. I drive a coupe."

I had to smile, envisioning Coal riding shotgun in a little two-seater.

"Anyway," he continued, "I took him straight to the nearest shelter to unload him as fast as possible, just like Gerard wanted."

I thought of what Katie had told me when she'd tried to buy Coal. "But I heard there was a staff email that went out, asking if anyone could take in Gerard's dog."

"That was a ruse," the doctor said. "That's what I told Katie when she came asking for the dog—which of course, made me suspect she was involved in Gerard's death. I convinced her that her email must've gotten lost."

"Did you tell this to the police?" I asked.

"Showing interest in a coworker's dog is hardly proof of murderous intent," he said. "I figured if Katie was involved in whatever kind of transporting Gerard was doing, the police would turn that up."

"So why did you just now decide to text me?" I asked.

"Ah." He pushed off with his feet, setting his rocking chair going. "Because it was only when you and Katie were discussing how you'd adopted Gerard's dog and you said it had been stolen that I put two and two together. I didn't have time to talk with you that evening, so I asked you to meet me tonight."

"So what, you just wanted to confirm that I'd adopted Gerard's dog, or you wanted to know if he'd been found yet?"

"Oh, no, I knew you'd found him—I overheard Katie talking at lunch, and she said she'd stumbled across Gerard's Great Dane in the golf shed. She told me you had him back, so I thought I'd tell you he must be worth something, given the way Gerard wanted to protect him."

I knew something the doc didn't seem to know—that the metal tag Gerard had hidden on Coal's collar was likely worth more than the Great Dane himself. But I wasn't about to play that hand. The doc may have *told* me Gerard found him trustworthy, but I was still suspicious of everyone who worked at Ivy Hill. Quite possibly, he was stealthily probing me for information.

"I see." I brushed the leather flecks off my pants. "Yes, Coal —that's what I named Gerard's dog—is back, safe and sound, with me. Thank you for letting me know your concerns, Doctor, but I don't plan on ever selling Coal, no matter how much he's worth. However, I've already upped my vigilance with him and made sure my house is completely secure. I'll keep my eyes open when it comes to Coal, I can assure you."

The doctor stood, and I followed suit. He shook my hand.

"Good. I won't keep you any longer. I just felt I should tell you in person, and seeing as how you hadn't booked another counseling session yet, I wanted to let you know sooner rather than later that your dog might be valuable. I wondered whether he was some rare strain of Great Dane—something worth a lot for stud fees, that kind of thing."

Summer had said that Coal was fixed, so he wasn't going to be hired out as a stud, but I did need to follow up with a vet and get some more background on his overall health and make sure his shots were up to date. Summer had given me the names of the closest vets, but none had a record of Coal. I guessed I needed to widen my circle.

Making my way down the attic stairs in front of Doc Schneider, I asked, "Who did Gerard leave his things to, do you know? I'd like to see if they got Coal's vet records, or if they could at least direct me to the right vet."

"I don't think he had family to speak of," the doctor said. "In fact, I think Alice was the one who went through his house and got it ready for the market. I think she said she'd rented one of those storage buildings for his furniture? I could put a few feelers out with her, if you want."

"I'd love that." I opened the attic door, only to hear several people running up from downstairs. I hurried out and when the doctor emerged, I closed the door behind him. To cover for our secret attic meet-up, I managed to feign a conversation with him by the time someone topped the stairs.

I had my back to them, but the doctor gave an audible gasp and pointed.

Detective Hatcher, who wore jeans and a polo shirt, rushed into Alice's office with two uniformed officers close behind. The doctor and I inched closer to her office door. I wasn't prepared for what I saw.

Alice sat at her desk, her head dropped at a strange angle.

Her lifeless eyes were bloodshot and she had a bloody nose, as well. Police were gently tugging her blue scarf from her neck, and I realized it had been pulled tight.

"Strangulation," the doctor breathed.

I sat down on a nearby chair, stunned into silence. Detective Hatcher caught sight of me and stepped out of the office. "Miss Hatfield. Did you just come upstairs?"

The doctor was backing into his own office, but I wasn't sure why. We basically *were* one another's alibis. I wasn't about to lie for him.

"No, I've been up here for maybe..." I looked at my phone. "Maybe thirty minutes or so. In the attic. With Doctor Mark Schneider, there." I pointed to the psychologist and his face froze. Why was he suddenly a Nervous Nellie?

Detective Hatcher glanced at Doc Schneider. "So you and your psychologist were meeting in private because...?"

That was why Doc Schneider was nervous. Our meeting looked shady for reasons I hadn't thought of—reasons that might make his wife doubt his loyalty.

"We were discussing my dog—you know, the one that got dognapped. Doctor Schneider wanted to talk about how he'd transferred the dog to the shelter, but there were a few details he wanted to keep private from the staff at Ivy Hill."

The detective looked dubious, but he was obviously distracted by the flurry of activity in Alice's office. "Okay. Did you happen to notice anything unusual when you came upstairs? Someone lurking around Miss Stevenson's office, perhaps?"

"Oh, no, there was no one upstairs when I got here, around a quarter to eight. Although I did notice Alice's office door was wide open and her light was on, which seemed strange with so many guests around." I took another quick glance into the office and realized something had changed. "Wait—she had a lamp on her desk when I came up, and I don't see it now. It was pretty and had dragonflies on it." I stepped a bit closer. "And those drink glasses on her desk weren't there before. Maybe she was talking to someone in her office?"

Detective Hatcher nodded, making note of what I'd told him. "Did you have anything to add, Doctor Schneider?"

The older man anxiously shook his head. "I didn't pay attention, but I think Alice's door was closed when I came upstairs. I went straight up to the attic. That was maybe five minutes before Macy arrived."

"All right, thank you for answering my questions." The detective headed back toward Alice's office, then gave an abrupt turn and pointed at both of us. "Oh, and you know the drill—don't go out of town and all that. We might need to talk with you some more."

Doctor Schneider paled and nodded. "You can reach me here at Ivy Hill," he said.

When the detective disappeared into Alice's office, a shiver went up my spine. I turned to the doctor, who was shuffling into his office. "Hang on—is he saying that we're suspects?" I asked.

"It would appear that way." The doctor gave me a rueful look. "Perhaps a secret meeting wasn't the best idea I've ever come up with. But I figured it would be more discreet than meeting in my office on the night of a community party." He nervously tugged at his tie. "You see, I had an...indiscretion early in my marriage, and I've worked hard to rectify things with my wife. It wouldn't have looked right if she came to my office and found me with you, since you're a pretty young woman and all."

I froze up, although I managed to say, "I understand." While I could tell his compliment was well-intended, I felt myself grow cold toward the friendly psychologist. I had thought he was lending a sympathetic ear when I told him about Jake's affairs, but maybe he was just a selfish philanderer like my ex. My lips gave a little twist of disgust.

The observant doctor rushed to reassure me. "As I said, it happened when I was very young, and I've definitely owned up to my own stupidity. I've never lapsed again, and I don't intend to. Thus my precautions tonight."

I murmured again that I understood and said an awkward goodnight. As I headed downstairs, I wondered how the doctor's wife had forgiven him...and if she would ever truly forget.

18

I WALKED outside the building and into a frantic hubbub. Police officers were taking guests' names and numbers before requesting they clear out. The oyster fire had died down, and guests were clustered in groups, murmuring about the murder. News had spread quickly.

In the largest group of people, I spotted Isabella, who was talking animatedly with Katie. Moving closer, I caught the tail end of their conversation.

"You were the one who found Alice?" Isabella asked Katie. "What did she look like?"

Katie grimaced and seemed to blink back tears. The masseuse sure had a way of turning up at crime scenes, I'd give her that. First, she'd discovered Coal barking in a remote golf shed, and now she'd stumbled onto Alice's body in her office? She was the one the cops needed to haul in for questioning.

Mary Anne clasped Isabella's arm, as if to steady herself. "Oh, don't let's talk about such gruesome things, Izzy."

Isabella glanced at her distressed friend, giving her hand a comforting pat. "Of course, darling." Smoothing her sleek blonde hair, her gaze flickered over the group. "Now, where did that man of mine get to?" She looked at Mary Anne's husband. "Peter, have you seen Glen?"

Mary Anne's husband shook his head. "Not since he finished his oysters. He said he was going to sit by the fire and enjoy the night air. That was maybe half an hour ago?"

Isabella gave a delicate huff and stalked off in her high heeled leather boots, which were a bit over the top for an outdoor event like this.

Katie's eyes were still widened with apparent shock, and she glanced from side to side as if unsure how to escape the failed oyster party. She could have a guilty conscience...or she could have genuinely been close with Alice, which seemed the more likely conclusion given her obvious distress. She probably wouldn't recover quickly from stumbling onto her strangled boss. I had only seen Alice from a distance, but for Katie to see her staring, reddened eyes up close and realize she was dead would've been horrifying.

Just when I was about to take mercy on her and lead her from the crowd, Jedi moseyed over to her and pressed a bottle of sparkling water into her hand. He murmured something in her ear and wrapped an arm around her, leading her toward the main building. In that moment, Jedi actually seemed human, instead of a kind of caricature.

The crowd had thinned considerably, and I decided to get out before the roving police officers asked me more questions. I was halfway to my car when Dylan came jogging up to my side.

I'd been so distracted, I had actually forgotten he was at the party.

"Macy, what happened? I saw you come out of the building, then the cops were asking questions about Alice...what's going on?"

"Alice was murdered." The words came out colder than I'd

intended, since I was still mentally kicking myself for meeting up with Doc Schneider one-on-one.

He slowed. "Murdered? How? Why?"

"I don't know. The whole thing seems weird. I mean, the glasses, the lamp—"

"What do you mean?"

I hit the button to unlock my car door. "It's just that when I went upstairs—I had to do something up there—I noticed this pretty dragonfly lamp on her desk. Then later, when her body was found, the lamp was missing and there were these two drink glasses sitting on the desk where they hadn't been before." I knew I was rambling, but Dylan gave an encouraging nod for me to continue. "I mean, the lamp hadn't been used to bash her on the head or anything, even though the base would've been heavy enough to do that. She was strangled, Dylan. It was awful."

He took a moment to process what I was saying. "So the lamp was missing after she was killed, but it wasn't used to kill her."

I nodded, sitting down in my driver's seat because I was weary of standing. I left my car door open.

Dylan leaned against the car frame and peered in at me. "That lamp—you said it had dragonflies and a heavy base? How close did you get to it? Can you describe it for me?"

I wasn't sure why he was so interested in the lamp, but talking about it took my mind off the vision of Alice that kept playing out in my head. "Not very close, but sure. It was this green stained glass shade with big dragonflies, and their wings overlapped on the ends. There was some kind of metal used for the top of the lamp and for the kind of twisty base—it looked like copper, but maybe it was brass? And I think there was a swirl of that green glass in the base, too. All in all, it looked heavy." I began to speculate aloud. "Do you think the killer had to hide it for some reason, maybe DNA evidence? There's no way they could've carried that out without getting noticed," I mused.

Dylan seemed to be hyperventilating. He snatched his phone from his jacket pocket and typed something, then flipped the screen out so I could see it.

Pointing to a picture of a lamp that could have been the same one I saw, he asked, "Was it kind of like this?"

"Yes! It was nearly exactly like that," I said.

His pupils widened and he jabbed at the screen. "Macy, this is a Tiffany lamp. It's worth somewhere in the neighborhood of one *hundred thousand* dollars."

"Well, that explains why the murderer didn't bash Alice in the head with it," I said.

Dylan's face still registered complete surprise. It was as if an art find of this magnitude sent him reeling.

I leaned on my steering wheel, wishing I could be home already. "So they must've killed her to steal the lamp. But why did Alice have a hundred thousand dollar lamp sitting smack dab on her desk, just as pretty as you please?"

"It certainly wasn't part of her decorating budget," Dylan said darkly. "She never mentioned owning a lamp like that, or I would've advised her to decorate her office around it."

"Maybe it was a new addition," I said. I made a mental note to ask Bo if he'd seen it when he'd inspected the room during our Thrive at Life class.

I was ready to get home to Coal, who was no doubt languishing in my absence. "I'd better get going," I said. "Don't worry—I'll call the police and let them know that a Tiffany lamp went missing from her office."

Dylan nodded. "Good. I'll check in with my fellow gallery owners, see if there's any buzz that a lamp like that was stolen lately."

We agreed to text each other if we found out anything. My goodbye was lackluster, to say the least, but I was in no mood for flirtation. Alice had been killed, and it was likely connected with the lamp I might've been the only one to see.

I PARKED under a streetlight and walked up to my house. A man in a hoodie jogged toward me and I shoved my hand in my pocket, palming my knife.

"Sis," he called out, and I realized it was Bo, taking a very late run.

"What're you doing out at this hour?" I asked, opening my gate.

He pounded up to my side, not even winded from his exertion. "I could ask you the same question, Miss I'm Staying Home to Watch Movies Tonight.'"

I sighed. "You might as well come in. I went to Ivy Hill for an oyster roast—long story—but some things happened and I want to talk them out with you."

Bo followed me into the house, where Coal nearly knocked me down with his exuberance. After hanging my jacket in the closet, I came back into the kitchen to find Bo rummaging in the fridge.

"I'm hungry," he said plaintively. "I'll make us some grilled cheese and tomato soup."

That was Auntie A's favorite comfort food—the thing she'd always fix when we were coming off a stomach bug. My brother could tell I was rattled.

I thought about Bo's late run. "*Wait* a second...you weren't patrolling outside my house, were you?"

He shrugged, his back to me as he buttered the bread. "Maybe."

I rolled my eyes. "I can take care of myself. Case in point, I was at the scene of a murder tonight and I didn't get killed."

He whipped around. "A murder? At an oyster roast? Explain yourself."

I elaborated on the events of the day, starting with my mystery text from Doc Schneider and working my way up to Alice's strangulation. Then I shared about how Dylan and I had worked out that Alice had a Tiffany lamp on her desk that went missing after her murder.

By the time I wrapped up my tale, Bo had finished making the food. Grabbing our plates and bowls, we made our way to the table and sat down. Coal followed me over and sprawled on the floor a respectful distance away. Although he eyeballed every bite that moved toward our mouths, he didn't beg.

"So, let me get this straight," Bo said. "Alice was boldly displaying a hundred thousand dollar lamp on her desk before she was killed." He pointed his spoon at me. "It had to be a new lamp, mind you, because it wasn't there when I checked her office the other night."

"I was going to ask you that," I nodded and took a bite of my sandwich. It was perfectly toasted on the outside, the cheese melted and gooey on the inside.

Bo continued. "And she left her office door wide open during a huge party."

"Right. At the time, I thought it was really strange, especially if she stored the center's money in there."

He sipped a bit of soup. "Do you recall Alice leaving the oyster roast?"

I thought back. "She made an introduction, then she asked guests to sign up for the center's email because they had some kind of updates they couldn't share yet...do you think that had something to do with the lamp?"

"Hard to tell," Bo said. He glanced at Coal, who was practically salivating as Bo brought his sandwich to his mouth.

"Gerard trained him well," I said, then stopped short. Gerard. Gerard was the missing piece of this puzzle. "Bo, remember how Gerard and Alice were allegedly arguing over something? What if it was the lamp? And remember that rhino horn story...I mean, why would Isabella make something like that up? What if there *was* an actual rhino horn on Alice's desk for a short period of time? Hang on, I'm going to ask Dylan what that would be worth."

I shot a text to Dylan, mentioning the carved rhino horn we'd heard Alice had at one time and asking what a real one would be worth.

His response was fast: *"They could go anywhere in the 300,000 dollar range if they have older carvings. I looked it up after our date, because I found it so hard to believe Alice would've gotten her hands on one."*

And therein was the problem—Alice had items in her office at various times that were likely worth more than her job paid in a year. How?

I reported Dylan's rhino horn estimate to Bo and he whistled. "They had to be black market—likely stolen goods. Do you think Gerard or Alice were thieves?"

I thought about what Gerard had told Doc Schneider. "He said he was transporting things for someone," I said. "I'm betting he wasn't the mastermind behind this. Alice must've been in on it, too...maybe storing items in her office until someone could pick them up?"

"And they might have fought over their cut of the cash?"

Coal's head bobbed from Bo to me as we spoke. He was obviously still hoping for a tiny bite of food, but I didn't want him to get used to eating table scraps. I jumped up and grabbed a doggie treat, which he tugged from between my fingers and swallowed in one delicate move.

"I don't even think he chewed that," Bo marveled.

"I know." I walked over to the stove. "I'm making hot water for tea—do you want some?"

"Sure, do you have any of that oolong left?"

"Sure do." I busied myself brewing a pot of tea, hoping my imagination would fill in the blanks on the art fencing operation.

But Bo's brain was whirring along faster than mine. "She was hiding things in plain sight," he said, his voice tinged with wonder. "She didn't think anyone would recognize the value of her office decor...and they didn't."

"Except Isabella," I said. "She glimpsed the carved rhino horn and was the first to tell the world about it. Or at least her bestie, Mary Anne." I set a couple of mugs and spoons on the table and took the lid from my sugar bowl.

"But didn't you say she was talking about it at Barks & Beans? Not exactly a private venue, you know? Maybe someone other than Mary Anne and you overheard her."

I poured the golden tea into our mugs and stirred sugar into mine. "I can't remember who was there that day, because that was right after we opened. But Isabella did have loose lips, talking on about Gerard and how wonderful he was and how weird Alice's office decor was..."

Bo blew on his tea and finally took a hesitant sip. "This is worth following up on, for sure."

"I planned to call Detective Hatcher in the morning," I said. "It's too late tonight."

"He's still wrapping up a murder scene, so I'm sure he's awake. But I'll be happy to make a few calls, too," Bo said seriously.

I laughed at his important tone, nearly snorting tea up my

nose. "Who are you going to call? The president of the coffee company?"

Bo's blue eyes met mine. "Actually, that's exactly who I'm going to call." He paused, studying me as if trying to decide if he should expound on his cryptic response.

"I don't get it—what do you mean?" I asked. Sure, I was on edge from the events of the night, but there didn't seem to be any way the coffee company could be involved in things.

Bo gave a slow nod as if he'd reached a decision. His eyes didn't leave my face. "Now I'm going to tell you something kind of shocking, something I haven't told anyone, so I need you to stay calm."

I instantly sobered. I'd only heard Bo use this particular tone a few times in my life, and each time, the news he'd shared had turned my world upside down.

"I'm listening," I said, taking a steadying drink of tea.

"The president of Coffee Mass is actually my boss, but not in the coffee company. Coffee Mass is a front."

"A front for smuggling!?" I shouted. Coal gave an anxious yip and loped over to my side, pressing his body against my thigh.

Bo gave a vigorous shake of his head. "No, of course not. Nothing like that." He grinned. "Don't you know I'm one of the good guys?"

I could hardly sit still. Waving my hands about like a hyper cheerleader, I said, "Well, what is it then? Tell me *right now!*"

"We're DEA agents, sis." He kept his eyes on my face, waiting for my reaction.

I felt like someone had sprayed my entire body with liquid nitrogen. My lips were frozen shut and I couldn't offer any response.

Correctly taking my silence as his cue to explain, Bo said, "Coffee Mass is a vehicle that allows us to develop a network with overseas coffee growers. Drugs and arms dealers often hide their products in coffee shipments, so it's important to have informants on the inside. What you and Auntie A didn't know is that soon after I got out of the Marines, I joined the DEA."

Suddenly, a lot of things swam into focus for me. "All those times I called at work and you didn't pick up?"

He nodded. "I was often doing recon work in other countries. Having a California home base worked well, since it gave me some distance from your questions. Any missed calls could be chalked up to the time zone difference, long work hours, that kind of thing."

"So you played me," I said bitterly.

Bo frowned. "No, sis. I *protected* you. You didn't need to know what I did."

"Are you still a DEA agent?" I had a hundred other questions where that one came from.

"Short answer is no, I'm out of the DEA—retired early, which is why I can tell you now."

"So was Tara really the reason you left your job?" I knew it was a personal question, but I needed to know.

"Yes, she was," Bo said. "I couldn't work with Tara anymore, thanks to the liar who set me up. After a lot of sleepless nights trying to figure out what happened, I believe one of the arms dealers I was getting close to set me up. He knew that a breakup with Tara would effectively derail me because I had to work with her every day."

My tea was getting cold, but I took a gigantic swig of it, finally tasting the sugar that had sunk to the bottom. "You mean they do that kind of thing? Interfere with your personal life like that?"

"Not typically, but this dealer is more...let's say *sadistic* than most. He felt I needed to be stopped, and he probably had me followed and discovered how important Tara was to me. I'm just thankful he didn't put out a hit on her."

"Or you," I said. Tears welled up, and I rubbed at my eyes to try to hide them.

Respecting my distress, Bo picked up our dishes and carried them to the sink. "Listen, I'll contact my old boss and find out who needs to be made aware of a possible fencing operation—besides the local P.D., of course. Why don't you call Detective Hatcher tonight and let him know what you figured out?"

My stomach sank. "Oh, sure, well...I still think tomorrow will be better—"

"What are you hiding?" Bo closed the dishwasher and looked at me. "You're hedging, Macy."

I stood and Coal did too, his tail thudding against my leg. I stepped forward to avoid the unintended beatdown and petted his head.

"I was near the scene of the crime," I said wearily. "I'm a suspect, Bo."

19

"You can't mean that," Bo said. "No detective in his right mind would suspect you."

"I was meeting with the doctor on the sly," I said. "It does look shady, if nothing else."

Bo plopped down on the couch. "You told the detective why you were meeting Doctor Schneider. You told him the truth about seeing Alice's office door open and what you saw missing from the crime scene—and what was new. I don't think you have to worry, sis."

I glanced at the clock. It was nearly midnight and I hadn't even thought about tomorrow. "Bo, we have to get sleep because tomorrow's Taste of our Towns! We have so much to do!" I felt panicky.

He waved his hand. "Try to relax. I already set up the kennel at our booth. We'll just need to get all the coffee things set up in the morning, and Milo and Kylie will help with that. Charity will bring her pastries, and Jimmy will be around to help you out. It's all under control."

I felt somewhat better, but not by much. It had been a ridiculous day all around.

Bo jumped up. "Right. I can tell you're zapped. Get straight to bed, and I'll meet you at seven. I know you were planning on six, but the event doesn't even start until eleven, and that'll give you a little extra time to sleep."

"Thanks, bro," I said, grateful for a slight reprieve. "Could you walk Coal, then lock up for me on your way out?"

"Of course, what are brothers for?" he asked.

I wanted to say *my* brother was good for subterfuge and busting drug smugglers, but I refrained. I was still smarting a little from the realization that he'd hidden his true job from me all these years, but at the same time, I understood why he'd done it. At least the truth had finally come out, and it might even help us figure out who killed Alice and Gerard.

I woke to find my feet were asleep because Coal had moved onto my bed in the night and stretched out across them. I tried to rub life back into them, enduring the tingling sensation that was necessary before I could move them again.

"Thanks a lot, big boy," I said, trying to glare at Coal. His winsome eyes were focused on me as if pleading for forgiveness, and when he inched closer to lick my hand, I gave in. I couldn't be upset with Coal for long. At every turn, he made it clear that I was his life and that he liked to see me happy.

Of course he was only a dog, but in many ways he was the exact opposite of my ex. Jake had lived for himself and only *pretended* he wanted to please me. In the end, the flowers and clothes and purses he bought were only ways to stroke his own ego with the consequent praise I gave him. It was embarrassing how grateful I'd been for the gifts that had meant nothing to him.

I sighed and pulled out a pair of dark denim jeans and a mint green shirt. It was one of my favorite colors because of how it set off my pale complexion with its sprinkling of freckles, and oddly enough, when I wore green, it made my eyes look more blue.

Thankfully, the humidity was lower and my hair looked somewhat stylish. Soon, I'd need to find a new stylist who knew how to work with thick waves like mine.

Summer called to say she'd bring the puppies straight to our booth, so I arranged to meet her there in thirty minutes. I went down and unlocked the interior cafe door. In the dog petting area, I gathered things I'd need to keep the pups occupied and stuffed them into a tote. It was clear that Bo had already been in to move coffee machines and cups.

Back at my place, I waited until Bo showed at seven. He was quiet—probably tired—so I didn't jabber as much as usually did.

Kylie came out to greet us when we arrived at our booth, and I was shocked to see that she wore jeans with no holes in them and a dress blouse that completely covered her dragon tattoo, except for the bit going up the back of her neck. She'd had her dark hair cut into a smooth bob, so instead of a biker babe, she looked positively French now. She wore her combat boots, but somehow they seemed to complement the look. As she helped Bo tote coffee items to the table, I made a mental note to ask who her hairstylist was.

Summer whizzed up in her car, popping out quickly with the pups on the leash. Both pups squatted in the grass to go to the bathroom.

"Sorry about that," she said. "They really don't have much bladder control at this stage."

We got them arranged with pillows and toys in the large kennel. Summer asked how Coal was doing, and I told her I'd finally located the vet Gerard had used—he was in another county—and they'd said Coal was up to date on shots and that he'd likely been fixed since he carried the gene for hip dysplasia, although thankfully, he wouldn't get it himself.

"That's a shame," Summer said. "He would've produced some gorgeous pups."

Jimmy arrived, and he and Summer fell into a conversation about the cows his father-in-law planned to show at the state fair next year. It shouldn't have surprised me how knowledgeable Summer was about cattle since she grew up Mennonite, but it did.

I worked alongside Bo and Kylie to get everything set up, and before long, Milo and Charity joined us. Bo demonstrated how to make a special maple syrup latte for the day, and Charity unveiled her goodies, which included more of the éclairs Alice had put in a request for. I felt a pang of sorrow that the center director had never gotten over to the cafe to taste one —whether she'd been an art fencer or not, everyone should get a chance to taste a really great éclair before they die.

As eleven o'clock rolled around, the town started humming with business. Bo was right—the streets were packed. Milo had to make more than one trip back to Barks & Beans to pick up extra supplies.

Detective Hatcher strode by, and Bo waved him over. I had texted the detective late last night about the possibility of Alice's involvement in a fencing ring, but he hadn't texted me back. Which meant he still probably considered me a suspect. I sank onto the folding chair I'd set up behind the puppies' kennel, hoping he wouldn't notice me.

No such luck.

"Miss Hatfield," the detective said, tipping his baseball cap.

He was once again wearing jeans, so I figured he wasn't on duty today. Or else he was on plainclothes duty...I glanced at his beltline for a gun, but it was covered with a loose leather jacket.

"Hi there, detective," I said, false cheer in my voice. "Care for a cup of coffee or a pastry?"

"I'd love one of those maple lattes," he said. "And maybe a chocolate chip scone?"

"You got it," Bo said, getting to work. He dropped his voice. "Any updates on the Alice Stevenson situation?"

Detective Hatcher stepped closer to Bo. "Your friend called me this morning. He had some great leads and we're following up with his sources."

Thank goodness for Bo and his connections! That must mean Alice *had* been involved in fencing stolen artwork.

"But we have another strong lead," the detective continued. "There's a person of interest, and we can place him in Alice's office last night. We've picked him up for questioning."

I blew out a silent sigh of relief. They'd picked someone up for Alice's murder, and it wasn't me.

20

Bo DRIZZLED maple syrup over the top of the detective's coffee. He didn't believe in stirring lattes, because he said layering the flavors made them all the more enjoyable. He popped a plastic lid on the cup and handed it to Detective Hatcher. His head tilted as he leaned in toward the detective. "Can you say who you picked up?"

The detective hesitated and glanced around. "Given your kind of clearance and your helpfulness in bringing the fencing to my attention, I can." Once again, my unassuming appearance was working in my favor, because Detective Hatcher didn't even seem to notice me. Although he spoke quietly, I was able to overhear what he said. "It's Glen Rhodes—a local and very successful businessman."

Glen Rhodes?

Isabella's husband.

Why on earth would he want to bump off Alice? Unless he were part of the fencing ring...

The detective stepped behind the table, leading Bo into the grass behind me where no one was milling around. I had to strain to hear what he was saying over the live banjo music that had kicked up in the background.

"We found evidence at the scene," Detective Hatcher continued. "Rhodes' prints and DNA were all over the second drinking glass. We also found Alice's phone and tracked down her messages. She'd been in private contact with Mr. Rhodes for several months. But that wasn't the only evidence." He took a long sip of his latte, rubbing his lips together to wipe off the foam. "Alice had recorded a phone conversation between herself, Glen Rhodes, Gerard Fontaine, and a well-known smuggler. Possibly she was recording it as insurance for herself...or blackmail."

Bo asked, "Do you know why someone murdered Gerard? Or who?"

Taking another sip, the detective scanned the area again. There was no one within earshot except me, and I kept feeding treats to the puppies as if I had no interest in the conversation.

"Since he was definitely in the fencing ring, we suspect he was holding out on them, maybe taking a cut on the side. We're going through Alice's computer and files, hoping to find a list of the artwork they transported. It's possible Gerard took something for himself and hid it."

I immediately thought of Coal's metal tag, but I'd already turned that over to the police, and they hadn't seemed to figure out its significance yet.

I had to pipe up. "Have you checked out the storage building Alice was renting?"

The detective gave me a curious look, like he was surprised to find me there. "We weren't aware she was renting one," he said slowly.

"Doctor Schneider mentioned she was storing Gerard's furniture and belongings in a storage building. Maybe you should look into that."

He nodded. "Thanks, Miss Hatfield. Will do—although we did go through Gerard's house immediately after his death, when all his things were there." He gulped his last bit of coffee and dumped the cup in the trash. "Thanks again, Mr. Hatfield. And both of you, please keep us posted on anything else that might be of interest in the investigation, okay?" After a parting chin lift, he wandered over to the next booth, handed them a token, and picked up a wooden skewer of shrimp and veggies.

Bo and I exchanged looks, but didn't have time to debrief as a new wave of customers descended.

A bounce house was set up not far from us, which was ideal, because several children made a pit stop at our booth. It didn't take long for both puppies to be spoken for. I referred the other interested parents to the shelter, feeling like I'd earned my keep today.

Around 2:30 as the event was winding down, Mary Anne and her husband dropped in. They were walking hand in hand, as if soaking up every moment of their lives together. Mary Anne ordered a hot chocolate and her husband purchased a couple of monster cookies.

She caught sight of me and waved, so I stepped over to her.

"How are you? How is Isabella? I saw both of you at the oyster roast," I explained. "I can't believe what happened to Alice Stevenson."

Mary Anne gave me a dubious look, as if uncertain of my relationship with Isabella. She had every right to be unsure—after all, I'd only talked to the woman a few times and I certainly didn't run in her circles. But the need to gossip won out.

Clinging to her cup of hot chocolate, she said, "It's been awful for Isabella, I'm sure. Her husband was taken down to the police station for questioning, can you imagine?"

Mary Anne's husband stepped closer. "Glen Rhodes has

been a fixture in this town for years," he added. "I can't see how he even knew Alice Stevenson."

Mary Anne shook her head. "Now honey, I've told you this. Glen's company donated money to Ivy Hill on a regular basis." She smiled at me. "Trying to do good in the community, you see."

I nodded. "Of course."

Mary Anne frowned. "I did tell the truth, though, when the detective asked me about Glen and where he'd been during the roast. I mean, I couldn't lie, could I? I told them he'd wandered over to the fire a while before the cops showed up and we couldn't find him afterward." She blew on her hot chocolate. "Then I found out Isabella told the cops that Glen had gone up to the main building with her at one point, but they'd both come straight back to the roast. Of course, she was lying for him."

Mary Anne's husband piped up. "Isabella doesn't come from money. Without Glen's income, she'd be sunk."

Mary Anne shook her head at her husband. "Now, Peter, you're being overly harsh. Isabella can get a job if Glen winds up in prison. She worked for years before she met him—I think she was actually a high school history teacher. It wasn't her favorite work," she added as an aside to me.

"Is Glen back home?" I asked.

"I haven't heard yet," she said. "Isabella keeps forgetting to update me, poor thing."

The line was growing in front of the table as people made a last-minute rush for goodies. Mary Anne and Peter moved toward the next booth.

"It was nice to see you," I called after them. "Thanks for stopping by."

Mary Anne nodded and her husband pulled a handful of

tokens from his pocket, ready to prolong the food-tasting adventure.

I was packing up puppy items when I heard a familiar voice. "How's it going today?"

Dylan walked up behind me, looking somewhat the worse for wear after last night's oyster roast. He had circles under his eyes and his clothes and hair looked rumpled.

"Long night?" I asked as one puppy began jumping up and down.

"Yeah," he said, his voice a little hoarse. "I was up late, trying to track down that missing Tiffany lamp, and I think I found it. One was stolen a few months ago in Vienna. The owner swore it was an inside job—he thought one of his employees took it."

"It looked like the one I described?"

"Exactly," Dylan said.

I was about to tell him about the fencing ring—and it *was* a ring, if Gerard, Alice, and Glen Rhodes were all involved—but I felt a strange hesitation. I distracted myself by petting the puppies, trying to figure out the cause of my unease.

And then it hit me—where had *Dylan* been during the oyster roast? I'd seen him early in the evening, then he hadn't turned up again until we were walking to the parking lot.

"Uh, yeah, well, you should tell the cops about that," I said vaguely.

His eyes searched my face and disappointment flooded his features. "Last night, you seemed eager to figure out why Alice was killed. I was only trying to help you out."

My instincts were screaming at me so loudly, I could hardly respond. Thankfully, Bo came over and clapped Dylan on the back. "Come over and try one of these maple lattes before we close up shop," he said. "It's on the house for our cafe design consultant."

Dylan gave a wan smile and followed Bo to the table. I

turned back to the puppies, trying to conceal my chaotic thoughts. I couldn't deny the facts in front of my face.

It was a fact that I hadn't seen Dylan after the very start of the oyster roast, and that he was nowhere in sight when the police showed up. Of course, I was in the attic part of the time...but Dylan would've had ample opportunity to get in and out of Alice's office, then maybe hide somewhere in the sprawling building until the crowd started breaking up.

It was a fact that Dylan, of all people in this town, would've known exactly what a rhino horn or Tiffany lamp were worth...and perhaps he knew Alice, Glen Rhodes, and Gerard were fencing them. Or perhaps I'd tipped him off about the rhino horn on our date, and he'd decided to get a closer look by breaking into Alice's office. He could've discovered the Tiffany lamp, then strangled Alice when she walked in on him.

Or perhaps Dylan was the mastermind smuggler shipping fenced goods to Ivy Hill.

I shivered, shooting a glance at the table. Bo was deep in conversation with Dylan...wouldn't my brother, a DEA officer, have some kind of inkling if Dylan were crooked? Some kind of instinct he was untrustworthy? Yet Bo seemed to like Dylan, even to the point of giving him my cell number so he could ask me on a date.

I tried to talk myself down. Glen Rhodes had most definitely been in Alice's office the night she was murdered, and there was proof he'd been part of the fencing ring. His company had donated money to Ivy Hill, perhaps as a repayment for Alice and Gerard's risks in transporting the stolen goods? Glen was the dangerous one here. The cops would gather evidence and nail him soon enough. Dylan had likely been talking to guests last night, handing out flyers for his gallery, just as he'd said he was going to do.

I was getting a little paranoid, and I knew why. Ever since

Jake had cheated on me so flagrantly, assuming I'd never find out, I had a bad taste in my mouth toward men who seemed interested in me. It was quite possible I was attracted to liars.

Dylan finished his latte and walked back to me. "I'm sorry I mistook your rhino horn questions for a desire to dig deeper into Alice's motivations," he said. "Bo was telling me how exhausted you were last night after talking with the police, and I totally understand. We won't discuss that awful oyster roast again." He smiled. "If you have some night free next week, I'd love to take you to a little French restaurant. We can talk about kittens and puppies all night, if you like."

I returned his smile, appreciating his attempt to ease the awkwardness between us. "I'll let you know," I said. I wouldn't let my ex-husband hang-ups rule my life anymore.

But as Dylan walked away, I couldn't shake the feeling he was far too interested in that Tiffany lamp.

21

On Sunday morning I felt sluggish, so I was dragging through my makeup application when Bo gave me a call. "Sorry," I said when I picked up. "I'll be ready in about five minutes."

Bo was likely waiting for me in his truck. Our church wasn't far away—it was the same church we'd grown up attending—but somehow I always managed to get out the door late.

"Actually, I need to come in and chat about something Detective Hatcher just told me." There wasn't an iota of humor in his tone.

I gave a blink, which caused mascara to smear onto both brow bones. "Oh, sure. Come on over." I hung up and silently began to panic. Had they found something that pointed to me for some reason? I couldn't think of anything I would've done to implicate myself in Alice's murder—primarily because I hadn't done it.

Coal nudged my hand with his wet nose, as if sensing my dismay.

"It'll be okay, boy," I said, rubbing his smooth forehead.

Bo didn't waste a moment, unlocking my door just after I'd donned my jeans. I hadn't even bothered with a skirt, because I knew our churchgoing attempt was about to be completely derailed.

"What's going on—"

"Sis, we have to be careful. I won't beat around the bush— we have to fly under the radar. You know that arms dealer I was telling you about? The one who tried to torpedo my life when I got too close?"

"Yes, what about him? Why do we have to be careful?" My panic shot up a notch or two, and I could feel my pulse quicken.

"Because *he* was the smuggler involved in that conference call Alice recorded. I happened to think to ask Detective Hatcher for a name, and it was him. Leo Moreau."

Leo Moreau. The name brought up images of *The Island of Dr. Moreau*, a movie that had single-handedly destroyed the raging crush I'd developed on Marlon Brando in *A Streetcar Named Desire*.

"Now, the DEA is keeping tabs on him and he's not in West Virginia," Bo continued. "He's actually on a private island. But his tentacles are everywhere—he's obviously been running this fencing ring at Ivy Hill." Bo sat down on my couch, and I followed suit. Coal dropped onto the floor at my feet and angled his head our way, as if tuning into our conversation.

"I moved here to fall off Moreau's radar," Bo said. "He didn't realize I had any family left, because you and Auntie A weren't on any of my records. I deliberately buried any trails to West Virginia." He scrubbed at his beard. "I thought this would be the safest place to live. He took Tara from me and he also got the satisfaction of knowing I quit working at Coffee Mass. So now I have to ask myself if he somehow followed me here to set up shop, or if it's just a fluke."

I rubbed at my arms as a chill swept over me. "But haven't you talked with Tara on the phone? He could've had your calls traced."

"I've used a burner phone for all my California calls," he said. "I guess a simple online search could've turned up articles linking my name to the Barks & Beans opening, but I figured Moreau would've backed off once he knew he'd ruined my career."

"Maybe he has," I said hopefully. "Maybe it's just a coincidence that he has people smuggling in Ivy Hill." But I had to admit, that would be quite a coincidence.

"Maybe." Bo gave Coal's head a pat as the dog stood and did a full-body stretch in front of him. "I've called in a favor with a friend in the FBI, so they'll also be looking into Moreau's fencing business. Between them and the DEA, I don't think Moreau will be able to get close to us without our having a heads-up. And Detective Hatcher has been informed of our situation. But I need you to stay well away from Ivy Hill, sis. We've gotten too entangled with things as it is, thanks to Coal's dognapping." He shot my dog an apologetic look.

Coal misread Bo's direct eye contact and eased into a sitting position on the floor, as if he'd done something wrong. I smiled to realize the alpha dog in this room wasn't even a dog—it was my brother.

And my brother had always protected me. That's why he'd come straight over to warn me of Moreau.

"I'll stay well away from Ivy Hill," I assured Bo.

"Good." He shot me a brief smile. "I saw you and Dylan talking yesterday. I think he's definitely into you, given the way he kept turning to see what you were doing during our conversation."

Or he was trying to monitor my reactions, perhaps sensing I'd started to suspect him of being involved in the fencing ring. "Uh, yeah. I'm not sure if that'll go anywhere," I said honestly.

Bo patted my shoulder before jumping to his feet. "You'll find a good man someday, I know it. You deserve one."

"Right back atcha, bro—I know you'll find the right gal."

"How about I make us some tea?" he asked. "I could use a pot of Earl Gray myself."

"That sounds great." I absently stroked Coal's side, trying to make sense of the sequence of events. Gerard had been moving art pieces for a fencing ring and had been violently killed, but it wasn't clear why. Maybe he'd become a liability somehow? Maybe he'd let something slip to the wrong person?

Alice had boldly been hiding stolen art items in plain sight, but if she hadn't been strangled, I was betting no one would've been the wiser as to the real value of her eclectic and ever-shifting office decor.

Glen Rhodes had also been in on the ring—in what capacity, I wasn't sure, although he had been a monetary donor to Ivy Hill. All the evidence seemed to indicate that Glen had killed Alice. But if he was smart enough to participate in the fencing ring, why would he have made the rookie mistake of leaving a glass with his fingerprints on it at a murder scene?

Then there were the outlying suspects. Sure, Doc Schneider was with me when Alice was murdered, but what if he'd somehow cleverly constructed a way to strangle her just before we met, then had someone shift her into her office chair while we were in the attic? I would've provided him with an airtight alibi. He *had* seemed very nervous when Detective Hatcher had asked him to stick around in case of more questions.

Could Katie or Jedi have been working with the doctor? Or maybe one of them had acted independently and killed Alice.

Katie had seemed genuinely shocked to stumble onto Alice's strangled body, but that could've been a clever act. Katie had also located Coal in a very obscure corner of the golf course, which felt like more than just happenstance.

Jedi had avoided me on his latest trip to Barks & Beans, but maybe he was still smarting because I'd dropped his drumming class. I couldn't picture Jedi strangling anyone, but then again, maybe his hands were super strong from his avid drumming.

Bo handed me a cup of Earl Gray with cream and sugar. He'd poured it into one of Auntie A's favorite china teacups—a yellow Taylor and Kent pattern with a nosegay of cheery flowers just inside the rim. As the familiar bergamot flavor burst into my mouth, it felt like a hug from Auntie A herself.

"You're thinking about the murder, aren't you?" Bo eased onto the couch, his teacup rattling against the saucer.

"I am. Nothing seems to add up, that's all."

He shook his head. "That's just what I mean. You can't let your mind go there. Let the professionals look into it." He sipped his tea. "Detective Hatcher seems to be on top of things."

"Like he was on top of Coal's dognapping?" I asked, a touch of bitterness in my voice.

"That was different," Bo said. "We didn't have anything to go on—no ulterior motives that made sense. And we still don't know what really happened." He glanced at Coal, who had dropped his head to his paw and seemed to be drifting to sleep. "Shoot, Coal's the only one who knows who took him." Bo took the final swig of his tea and stood. "I'm going to get on home. Sorry to drop such bad news on you, but I promise I'll be right here to protect you, sis. I'm not going anywhere."

"You mean the same way you were there for me at the end of high school?" I immediately felt remorseful for saying such an insensitive thing. What I'd meant as a playful jab had come out sounding resentful and maybe a little angry. Bo had gone into the Marines after graduation, and I couldn't blame him. Yet some part of me apparently had, because my final years of high school had been rough without him, and something inside me held him partly responsible.

Bo looked like I'd sucker-punched him. "You never told me you felt that way."

I tried to laugh it off. "It's fine; I made it through without you. I made salutatorian, remember?"

No doubt seeing through my faux joviality, Bo's tone grew stern. "Remember Larry Romano in your eleventh grade class?"

I hadn't even been aware that Bo had known the name of my junior year stalker. "Yes, I remember him," I said, trying not to picture the hulking guy with body odor who had never tired of hitting on me.

"Remember that time he followed you to the mall and got you alone in the movie theater?" Bo asked.

Thankfully, I didn't know what he was talking about. "No, I don't."

Bo grinned. "That's because it didn't happen. My friends told me they'd seen Larry following you around, and it was obvious you weren't interested in him. I put the word out with my senior bros to keep Romano well away from you. My friend Joel caught sight of that punk trailing behind you in the theater line, and he realized Larry was planning to sit next to you."

I began to smile as realization dawned. "That must've been the time Joel came in and plopped down right next to me at the movies. I went home wondering if he had a crush on me."

Bo chuckled. "No, he was doing exactly what I'd told him to do. I tried to have a long reach, even from boot camp, sis." He leaned in and gave me a brief hug. "So trust me when I say I'm not going to let Moreau get anywhere near you."

I appreciated Bo's intentions, but protective as my brother was, I doubted he had the power to fight an international smuggler who'd already derailed his engagement and his job.

I sighed. My investigation into the Ivy Hill shenanigans was officially over.

22

Monday started out feeling very much like a Monday. Coal wouldn't get out from underfoot as I got dressed and ate a Pop-Tart for breakfast, so I put him out in the garden for a bit. Once his rowdiness toned down, I brought him back in the house before trudging over to the cafe.

Ready for a reviving espresso, I walked straight over to Kylie and asked for one. She ran a hand though her dark bob. "Milo didn't clean the filter last night, so it'll take a few minutes. Want a cup of fresh-brewed regular in the meantime?"

Drip coffee couldn't compare to espresso, but I was desperate. "Sure, hit me up."

While Kylie poured me a mug, I headed over to Summer, who had just arrived. She looked a little harried.

"How'd things go with the puppy adoptions?" I asked.

"Oh, that was great," she said, tightening the leash attached to a highly strung little dog. "The entire litter was adopted, actually." The little dog leapt into the air—reaching Summer's waist—and she glared at it. "I'm so sorry I had to bring this one today, but I thought maybe he could run off some energy in the petting area. Once again, I'm a little understaffed." Her dark eyes met my own, pleading.

"Of course," I said, unwrapping the leash and steering the now-yipping pooch into the petting area. I felt a sudden urge to be friendly to the beleaguered shelter owner. "How are you?"

Summer fell into step alongside me. "Uh—well, I'm pretty busy at work. Sometimes I don't know how we're going to make ends meet."

"I'm sorry," I said, tossing a ball to the tiny dog. He chased it down and pounced on it as Summer unleashed the other three dogs that were sitting calmly at her side. "Sometime we need to get together and talk more about your Mennonite upbringing—I find that fascinating. You certainly seem to know a lot about Angus cows."

She shrugged. "I've kind of put that era behind me, you know? But sure, I'd love to hang out."

I was just about to suggest we catch a movie when Bo walked in. Summer turned to see who had arrived, and her eyes lingered on my brother.

My eyes nearly popped out of my head when I saw who walked in behind him.

The woman with short dark hair gave the cafe an appraising once-over. Her high cheekbones drew attention to her luminous green eyes, and her fitted athletic wear accented muscles you could only attain through regular workouts.

I realized it was none other than Tara Rainey, my brother's ex-fiancée. She must've flown here from California...but why?

Tara gave Bo's arm a light touch before stepping toward the dog petting area. "How quaint!" she exclaimed. Looking over the dogs, her eyes scanned past me and landed on Summer, as if sensing the competition.

Annoyed that she had no clue who I was, I stood and extended a hand. "Hi, I'm Macy—Bo's sister."

My voice must've snapped Bo out of whatever spell he was under. "Oh, yeah, sorry," he said. "Tara, this is Macy. Macy, Tara Rainey."

Tara came closer and gave my proffered hand a brief but undeniably aggressive shake. "Macy, nice to finally meet you."

"Thanks." I gestured to Summer, who was close to my side. "And this is Summer Adkins. She's great with dogs and runs the local shelter."

Tara nodded at Summer. "Delighted to meet you."

An awkward silence followed until Kylie opened up the steamer and air whistled out.

"So, you flew all the way to West Virginia? I didn't know you were coming in." I gave Bo a reproachful look.

My irritation wasn't lost on Tara. "I didn't tell Bo I was coming," she explained. "I actually rented a car and showed up at his place this morning. I think I scared him half to death, ringing the doorbell before the sun even came up."

Bo gave a nervous laugh. "You sure did."

It was hard to get a fix on what Bo was thinking, but for all intents and purposes, the cat seemed to have gotten his tongue. Given Summer's restless leg-shifting, it was safe to say Tara's visit had put us all on edge.

"So, where are you staying?" I asked.

Tara shot Bo a quick glance. "I hadn't quite worked that out yet."

Surely she wasn't planning to stay with Bo? Didn't she know him at all?

While shuffling toward the door, Summer lifted a hand in an awkward wave to no one in particular. "Nice to meet you, but I'd better get back to the shelter."

Bo didn't even respond. I could've smacked him for allowing Tara to throw him into such a trancelike state.

It would be polite to ask Tara to stay with me, but I had no inclination to make that offer. The woman had spurned my brother's love, and frankly, I wished she'd kept her fit little hiney back in California.

I shot Bo one last quizzical look. "I need to get to work. Hope you have a good time in Lewisburg, Tara." Normally, I would've suggested local sightseeing destinations, but honestly I just wanted her to turn around and fly home.

"Of course. Thanks." She turned her full attention to Bo, as if our conversation had been nothing but a blip on her radar. "How about you make me some coffee?"

As she took Bo's arm and led him toward the coffee bar, I couldn't stop myself. "*How about you make me some coffee?*" I mimicked in a low whisper. The spotted dog closest to me trotted up and nuzzled at my hand. At least someone in this place was sensitive to my feelings today.

DOING his part to add to the doldrums of my Monday, the frisky little dog moved over toward a smiling customer's feet and promptly relieved himself, as if he hadn't just been out on a five minute walk. Apologizing profusely as I cleaned and disinfected the smelly mess, I wondered if this day could possibly get any stranger.

Of course, it could.

I clipped the leash on the errant doggie and led him outside, just to make sure he'd taken care of all his business. Familiar voices sounded on the sidewalk, so I moved toward the front fence, where I could see who was walking by.

Katie and Jedi were striding along, arm in arm. Katie held a takeout container, so apparently they'd gotten lunch in town. She stopped abruptly to adjust her shoe, so I ducked down behind the wooden fence slats. The dog gave a little yip and I shot it a furious glare.

"Have you talked to the doctor yet?" Jedi asked. "I don't think he's going to mind."

Katie groaned. "Of course he'll mind. You know he's going to want to take over."

"We'll just vote on it...you know, the democratic way." Jedi gave a not-so-pleasant laugh. "I'll talk to the new golf kid—he'll be easy enough to sway."

"I don't know. The cops will be watching our every move."

"Who cares? Let 'em watch. They aren't going to stick us with anything."

These two were thick as thieves. And it sounded like they *were* thieves, scheming to take over Alice's fencing operation. At least Doc Schneider didn't seem privy to the inner workings, as well as the dense new golf instructor.

Katie sighed. "I wish I'd gotten my hands on Gerard's dog. That could've been lucrative."

My mouth gaped open. So Katie admitted she'd tried to get Coal, but she hadn't managed to. She hadn't been the dognapper.

Pulling at my arm, the dog gave another yip. I tugged him closer and unhooked his leash so he could run. He tore off like a live firecracker had exploded behind him.

As Katie and Jedi started walking, I heard Katie mention my name, but I couldn't tell what she'd said. Then Jedi seemed to change the subject, sharing that Glen Rhodes was in custody now, although that was all I could catch.

Were they in league with Glen Rhodes?

Maybe I should call Detective Hatcher and let him know about the conversation, but it seemed there really wasn't anything solid to share. Glen Rhodes was clearly involved in the fencing operation up to his eyeballs, and he must be the main suspect in Alice's death, if they'd finally taken him into custody.

The dog finally skittered to a stop at my feet, his tongue hanging out as he panted. "You pooped yet?" I asked, clipping the leash onto his collar. I'd been outside too long and I needed to get back to work.

I was cleaning my hands at the sink Bo had thoughtfully installed in the dog petting area when someone walked up behind me. I whirled to see Tara, who was watching me steadily. Her unswerving, unapologetic gaze reminded me of a large cat...like a mountain lion.

"Macy," she said, offering me a smile that didn't reach her eyes. "Bo wanted me to see how you were doing over here."

Really? My brother sent his ex-fiancée to check up on my work?

"I'm just fine," I said. I was adeptly managing the fractious dogs, just like I had since the very first day Barks & Beans had opened.

"I can see that." Tara seemed oblivious to my irritated tone. "He wanted me to ask if you'd join us at his place after work. He's going to order Chinese."

The way she phrased things made it clear it wasn't *her* idea that I join them. Was she always this rude? I had no desire to spend any time with her while she was in town, but maybe Bo wanted me around so he wasn't alone with her? Or maybe he still carried some hope that I'd develop a friendship with his ex?

That was about as likely as Bo developing a liking for *my* ex. Tara had dropped my brother like a hot potato, without bothering to hear his side of things. Still, I owed it to Bo to eat supper with them and run interference, so he wouldn't wind up harking to Tara's beck and call.

Why had she really flown to West Virginia? I had a sinking feeling she was going to tell Bo how much he was needed at

Coffee Mass and sweet-talk him into moving back to the West Coast.

I channeled all my Southern politeness, giving her a warm smile. "Of course I'd love to have Chinese with you all. I'll come over at six." That would give them very little time together.

"See you then." She turned and strode toward the coffee bar, where Bo was adding flavoring to a coffee drink. The moment she walked behind the counter, he froze, as if he'd forgotten the next step in the coffee-making process.

As if on cue, the little dog barked and jumped on the spotted dog, tearing into its side with his sharp little teeth. I raced over and pulled him off, leading him directly into the kennel.

Taking a deep breath, I examined the spotted dog. Although he had a few spots of blood on his coat, I was relieved to see he'd only gotten a little scratch and wasn't seriously injured.

I pulled out my phone and called Summer. "Hey, gal, I think we have a problem."

Something told me that as far as problems went, the terrorist dog was only the tip of the iceberg.

23

I SHOWED up at Bo's house at six on the dot and gave my brother a hug. He was wearing a Henley shirt that sadly made his muscles all the more noticeable. He also had that kind of rumpled, little-boy-lost look about him tonight, which I was sure Tara found irresistible.

"Help yourself, sis," Bo said, gesturing to Auntie A's red Fiestaware plates and the Chinese food set out on the island.

As I picked up one of the familiar plates from our childhood, I wondered what Auntie A would've said about Tara. I haphazardly piled vegetable Lo Mein and General Tso's chicken into the middle of my dish, not caring if I looked like a hungry piglet. I was gearing up for a battle of sorts—the battle of keeping my brother's head screwed on straight.

Tara surprised me by piling her own plate equally high—and with beef and broccoli. I'd figured she was a vegetarian, but apparently not.

I settled at the table and Tara joined me, but I didn't meet her eyes. I was fairly certain my negative emotions would be written on my face.

Bo filled his plate and sat down. He murmured a brief prayer and we began to eat.

I looked at Bo and held his gaze. It was clear he had something he needed to tell me, but he didn't seem inclined to share yet.

Hoping he wasn't going to make an announcement about bailing on Barks & Beans and moving away, I tried to make small talk. "So, where are you staying, Tara?"

She balanced her chopsticks on her plate and took a drink of water. "I'm over at that bed and breakfast a couple of streets up."

How convenient. She was within walking distance of wrecking my brother's heart.

"And do you know how long you'll be staying?" I pressed.

Bo cleared his throat. "Tara came here to tell me something," he said.

I was sure she had, but I tried to stay cool as I looked at Bo. "You don't say."

He seemed to wait for Tara to pipe up, but she didn't. Finally, Bo said, "Tara got a note at work. She wanted to show it to me."

I'd finally reached my limit. "She flew across the country to hand-deliver a note?" My lips and face felt tight as I shot Tara a look.

"It was a threat," she said. She took another bite of beef like she was disinterested in my reaction.

"From Leo Moreau," Bo added. He shot a brief look at Tara, then focused on me. "He said congratulations on the opening of my new coffee shop."

Numbness seemed to travel up my arms. "He knows where you are," I breathed.

"That's not all," Tara said, her voice unnaturally light.

Did she think this was a joke?

I beamed a huge smile at her and leaned in. *"Please* enlighten me as to the extent of our impending doom."

Bo seemed to snap to attention as he noticed my near-volatile reaction. "Moreau threatened to take away everything I hold dear if I ever got involved in his business again. I have to believe he's found out about you, Macy."

Tara leaned back. "I flew here to warn you to be careful, because I figured he was somehow monitoring my calls and email."

I jumped from my chair, unable to sit still. "So you just decided to fly here and lead him straight to us?"

Bo stood and placed a calming hand on my arm. "He obviously already knew where we were, sis. Tara's warning note included a printed copy of the news article on our grand opening. Tara was trying to protect us."

Tara dabbed at her mouth with a napkin, and again I was reminded of a cat...a cat licking its paws.

"Why do you trust her?" I blurted. "Shoot, she could've concocted that note herself."

"How would I have known Moreau's name?" she asked calmly.

I jabbed a finger at her. "Because you're working with him!"

Tara's stare didn't waver, and she didn't even flinch.

Bo came closer and wrapped me in a hug, which effectively turned me into a blubbering pile of mush. "Let's not make hasty accusations," he said.

I knew I'd been quick to point the finger at Tara, but I felt like I had no compunctions left. "I want to go home," I sobbed into Bo's chest. Maybe if I got away from Tara, I could pretend we weren't being targeted by a psycho smuggler.

"Of course," he murmured. "I'll walk you back."

I didn't bother saying goodbye to Tara. I hoped she'd realize her stupid news had sent me into a tailspin and decide to leave town early.

Bo didn't talk until we got in the door and Coal had trotted up to my side. "It's going to be okay," Bo said. "The DEA is all over this. Tara turned the note over to them. They've assured me that Moreau isn't in the U.S. If he tries to come into the States, he'll get snagged."

"But you said yourself he has tentacles everywhere." I gave a sniffle and Coal pressed against my leg. "And with all this hubbub over Alice and Gerard, he's sure to be checking up on his fencing operation, maybe moving new people into place." Like Katie and Jedi.

"Maybe, but we're not involved with that business at Ivy Hill," Bo said. "As long as I steer clear of that, we should be fine."

I dropped onto the couch. "But meanwhile, this smuggling boss is having you watched? And probably me, too?"

Bo ran a hand through his hair, making his short bangs stand on end. "Possibly. But possibly not. He could've just been trying to scare us. I know it sounds like I'm oversimplifying things, but fear actually is his greatest weapon."

I knew I had to fight back the fear, but right now it was consuming me. "Okay, thanks for that pep talk," I said, as bravely as I could.

He gave me a quick hug. "Thanks for coming over. I'll see you in the morning. It's going to be okay." As he opened the door, he added, "Also, in case you were wondering, I'm not pursuing Tara or anything. That chapter of my life is closed."

When he pulled the door closed, I let out a huge breath. Perhaps I'd been even more afraid of losing Bo to Tara's wiles than I was of Moreau. Barks & Beans needed Bo here, and so did I.

Coal jumped up and planted his upper body on my torso,

leaving his lower half balanced on the floor. He gave my hand a delicate lick, then sniffed at my face.

"Thank goodness Bo is over her," I said, stroking Coal's long, soft nose. "Now if only the cops could wrap up these murder cases. I know I have to stay out of things, but..." I picked up my phone and scrolled down to Detective Hatcher's number. "It seems the police should know about Katie and Jedi's plans, doesn't it, boy? I mean, it's safer for everyone if no one can take over Moreau's operation. I'll just let him know what I overheard, then we can finally relax."

Coal nudged his nose into my hand, hoping for more attention. I shooed him away as Detective Hatcher picked up.

"Hi, Detective. I think I have some information you need to be aware of."

24

Summer showed up bright and early with two very calm, older dogs in tow, and I couldn't have been more thrilled. I wasn't up to chasing uncontrollable canines around today.

"Sorry about yesterday," she said. "It's sad, but I'm not sure if anyone's going to wind up adopting that dog. He attacks other dogs and he's not properly potty trained. He isn't so great with humans, either—he bit one of my workers yesterday evening."

"That's a tough situation for you," I said, leading the elderly dogs to the petting room, where they gratefully tucked into the doggie treats I handed them.

"I'd like to shift into a No-Kill shelter, but then I couldn't take in all the strays," she said. "We'd have to be more selective."

"It has to be so hard, deciding which animals to euthanize." That burden must not sit easy on Summer's shoulders.

"I grew up on a farm," she said. "I know it sounds harsh, but it is survival of the fittest there—you do what you can to care for animals, but you have to accept that you can't save them all. I actually look at euthanization as a mercy. Most of the pets who get on that list are incurably sick or have extreme aggression issues, things like that."

"Still, you must feel so helpless," I said, sitting to stroke one dog's ear.

Summer sat on a comfy chair. "Well, we do things proactively, too. We're really aggressive about helping our local vets get the word out on spay and neuter clinics. And we've started recruiting some private homeowners to foster animals that seem well-adapted to family life." She made a sweeping gesture around the petting area. "And don't discount the impact Barks & Beans has made on the shelter. I was running numbers a few nights ago, and we've had an almost fifty percent uptick in adoptions since we started placing dogs in your cafe. *Fifty* percent, Macy!" She beamed.

Bo walked over, carrying two take-out cups. "Fifty percent of what?" he asked.

A light blush dusted Summer's cheeks. "Your cafe has helped the shelter do more adoptions than ever before—we're up by fifty percent."

Bo smiled, genuinely happy. "That was the idea. I'm so glad to hear our plan to help the local animals has worked."

Summer shot him a mischievous look. "Now we just need to find a pet for *you*, Bo."

My brother laughed. "Macy's the dog person. I'm not really into pets." He seemed to become aware of the coffee cups in his hands. "Oh, I brought you ladies a couple of house blends. As I recall, you take yours black, Summer?"

She stood and took the cup he offered, her long fingers brushing his. "I do."

I squelched a smile as I took my cup from Bo. Summer's "I do" almost seemed a portent. I just knew this girl was right for my brother. Once Tara was finally out of the picture in California, I'd have to have a heart-to-heart with Bo.

TARA SHOWED up around nine and bought a lemon poppyseed muffin and coffee. Bo joined her at a table. I worked on brushing one of the dogs while surreptitiously observing their conversation.

"I'm sorry we had to meet under these circumstances," Tara said. "You know the boss—he's been texting me since I boarded the plane in California."

"No sleep for the weary," Bo quipped. He wasn't looking directly at Tara, so maybe he was making an effort to ignore her allure.

"I'll fly out at three." She fell silent.

Was she waiting for Bo to offer her a ride? Would he?

The silence was broken by the cafe door banging open. Jedi stalked in, drawing more than a few stares. The man looked unkempt, like he hadn't slept in a couple of days.

To my astonishment, he marched straight toward me. I caught a whiff of something skunky, so I had the fleeting but irrational thought that maybe a skunk had followed him in.

As Jedi fixed me with a glare, I noticed how red his eyes were. "What'd you say...did you talk with the cops? They told me someone from this place heard us talking 'bout something, and we were standing by that dog walk fence. Must've been you; you never liked me anyhow." His words came out slow and he shoved a hand in his oversized jacket pocket.

There was a sudden thud as Bo jumped Jedi from behind and pinned him to the floor.

"Give me your hands." Bo's tone was impossibly controlled but completely unyielding.

The drumming instructor slowly extracted each hand. As he exposed his palms, it was clear to see both hands were empty.

Bo turned toward the coffee bar and barked out an order. "Bring me some of that twine from the back room."

"On it, boss," Jimmy said. The large man brought out a wad of twine in record time. He held Jedi down while Bo tied his hands.

"I called 9-1-1," Milo offered, rising from a crouched position behind the coffee bar.

Bo leaned down toward Jedi. "You care to explain why you came into my cafe all stoned, thinking you were going to hash something out with my sister?"

Stoned. Of course Jedi was stoned. I'd known a few marijuana users in high school, but I hadn't seen any recently, so I hadn't put two and two together with Jedi's smell and behavior. With Bo's DEA training, he was able to spot that stuff right off.

"Man, it's not what you think. She told the cops something on Katie and me. They came around this morning, and now what's going to happen to my job?"

"Did you kill somebody?" Bo's voice was hard.

"Naw, man, I didn't kill anyone," Jedi whimpered.

"Then why are you so worried?"

Jedi must've thought he was whispering, but all the customers could hear as he confessed, "I've got a little side gig there at the center. It's not really medicinal, you know? So it's not on the books."

"You're selling marijuana at Ivy Hill?" Bo asked, pulling Jedi into a sitting position on the floor.

"Yeah." Jedi's eyes were still a little unfocused. "And growing a little too, but don't tell anyone, man."

Bo sighed. The door opened and a couple of uniformed officers came in. As Bo explained the events of the morning, one officer snapped cuffs on Jedi.

A tall blonde suddenly burst through the door and made a beeline for Jedi. Of course, it was Katie. Was she his partner in crime? It would certainly appear so, the way she leaned close and murmured something in his ear.

As the cops walked Jedi outside, Katie stood in the cafe, occasionally rubbing at her nose and wiping at tears.

I couldn't stay still. After flagging Jimmy down to ask if he could man the dogs, I walked over to Katie's side and led her to a more private table in the corner.

Unsure how to ease into a conversation about Jedi, I asked Katie if she'd like a cup of coffee. She said she'd prefer some strong tea, so I asked Milo to brew her a mug of our Scottish breakfast blend.

Katie looked at me. "So...were you the one who reported our conversation to the cops? Jedi figured it had to be you."

"Yes, I overheard you yesterday," I admitted, wishing the police hadn't let it slip that someone from Barks & Beans had reported them. "You said something about being democratic in taking over and that the cops couldn't stick anything to you. I assumed you were talking about Alice's fencing operation, maybe making plans for when things calmed down at Ivy Hill."

Milo broke into the conversation by carefully setting the tea, cream, and sugar on the table. He raised his eyebrows at me, probably wondering why I was sitting with someone who'd been kibitzing with a criminal.

Katie took time to pour a liberal helping of cream and several spoonfuls of sugar into her tea. She stirred, took a sip, and closed her eyes. "This is the best tea I've ever had." Sitting up straighter, she leaned in toward me. "Now listen, I don't know what you're talking about. Jedi and I were discussing how I could take over as director at Ivy Hill, not how we could take over some kind of fencing operation. Are you saying that Alice was involved in fencing, as in fencing stolen things? What kinds of things?"

Clearly, my overactive imagination had taken over and filled in the blanks without enough evidence. Of course Jedi and Katie were discussing who would step in as director at Ivy Hill now that Alice was dead. Katie seemed genuinely clueless about the illegal operations going on at the center... at least the ones Alice had been running. Apparently, Jedi had his own illegal business going on there, too.

I wasn't sure how much I should tell her, but it probably wouldn't hurt to disclose that Alice and Gerard had been involved in a fencing ring. Police would be scrutinizing Ivy Hill even more closely now that they'd heard about the marijuana.

"It was art fencing," I said.

"What? You're kidding." She began to drink her tea in earnest, so I idly glanced around. Bo was watching me closely from behind the coffee bar. I felt bad that I hadn't given him a huge hug for thwarting Jedi in his misguided attempt to confront me.

Tara was no longer seated at the table, and I felt a jolt of realization. Had she already gone to catch her flight? Not that I'd had any desire to say goodbye, but I hoped Bo was able to get some closure with her after the Jedi takedown was wrapped by the police.

"I guess I should've known," Katie said, clutching her teacup. "Around March, Alice started acting weird at our monthly business meetings. We all assumed it was because Ivy Hill was hemorrhaging money. We got donations, sure, but we just couldn't maintain enough staff for proper upkeep. Besides, Alice refused to modernize the place or offer more practical classes. Truth be told, my massages, the golf course, and Doctor Schneider's counseling were what paid the employees. Who knows how the bills were being paid—maybe Alice's art fencing was keeping us afloat?"

As convincing as Katie was, she had a little more explaining to do. "I also overheard you saying that you wished you'd gotten your hands on Gerard's dog because it would've been lucrative. What did you mean by that?"

Katie chuckled, but not cruelly. "Just what I said. Great Danes are worth something, and that one is a beauty. And quite frankly, I was strapped for cash when Doctor Schneider unloaded the dog at the shelter. He should've asked around and given others a chance to take him."

"Were you actually close to Gerard or not?" I asked. "Was that just an act?"

"An act," she said firmly. "I used that sob story in hopes that you'd give me his Great Dane. In reality, Gerard was always asking me out and I was always turning him down. He wasn't my type."

"Oh, really? Who is, then? Jedi?"

She gave a tinkling laugh. "No way. Jedi's more like a brother to me—a punk brother, really. He's always breaking rules and getting in trouble, but in the end, he's loyal, you know? I figured he'd be useful if I ever got the chance to take over Ivy Hill." She sobered. "But I *never* dreamed that opportunity would come at the other end of Alice's murder. Finding her was...it just shook me, you know? That someone could be killed right there, in the middle of a public party like that?"

"But Gerard was murdered, too—out in the open."

She nodded. "Yes, but that seemed more removed from us somehow. I figured it was some disgruntled golf client who'd whacked him—something personal, you know? He *could* be blunt and grating sometimes."

"It did seem extremely violent," I agreed. "Was Gerard

going out with any of his clients? Would any of them have a reason to kill him?"

"None that I can think of," Katie said, finishing off her tea. "Gerard really acted like he wanted to date me, but like I said, I shot him down every time." She stood. "I need to get back to the center and update Doctor Schneider on what's happened with Jedi."

"Of course," I said, standing and picking up her empty teacup. "Thanks so much for chatting. I just had a lot of questions, especially given Jedi's behavior today."

"He was out of control," she acknowledged. "I'm so sorry he scared you all. Sometimes he doesn't have a filter with his emotions—especially when he's been doing pot, as you can imagine." She took a deep breath. "If I take over at Ivy Hill—or even if Doctor Schneider does—we'll have to let Jedi go. But I want him to get help with what's apparently become an addiction."

"I'm sure the doctor can help you with that," I said, giving her hand a brief squeeze. "All the best as you try to get Ivy Hill up and running again." I genuinely meant it, too. Katie seemed to be a smart woman who had lots of good ideas for the spiritual center. Maybe she could implement them and really make a difference in the community at large.

Once Katie left, I went directly over to Bo and gave him a hug. "If he'd been armed, you would've saved my life."

Bo let go of me and grabbed the whole milk from the mini fridge. "It's just a regular day in the neighborhood for me, sis. I'm used to looking for behavior like that—you aren't."

"You're a guard dog, I get it," I said. "I saw you watching me talk with Katie just now."

"Not for the reasons you might think." He frothed the milk and poured it over espresso, using a toothpick to create a whimsical leaf design on top. "Doesn't she work at Ivy Hill, too? I told you, we have to stay well away from that place."

I put a hand on my hip and took a step back. "Well, today Ivy Hill came to me, didn't it?"

Bo gave me a serious look. "That Jedi guy said you'd informed on him to the police. I'm just wondering if that happened *before* or *after* I'd talked to you about the importance of lying low to stay off Moreau's radar?"

Ugh. He had me there.

"After, but I overheard them on the sidewalk yesterday and I wanted to make sure the police had all the facts."

"Strong moral compass you have there," Bo said, handing the mug over to an older woman with a smile. I noticed she was wearing lipstick and a fancy scarf—obviously she was out on the town today.

I cupped a hand to my mouth and whispered. "Did Tara leave?"

Bo nodded. "She left right after the police came. She had a rental car."

I tried to probe Bo's steady blue gaze for any hints of emotion. "Did you get to say goodbye?"

He grabbed a clear plastic cup to fill an iced coffee order. "I did." He gave a half-smile. "I'm fine, sis."

Milo edged around Bo and leaned in toward me. "You okay?" he asked, his tone unusually serious. "That was awful! If they want to keep kids off drugs, they just need to show them live, unfettered exhibits like that dude. No way I'm doing marijuana."

I couldn't restrain my grin. "I'm glad a valuable lesson has been learned today. Thanks for calling in help, Milo."

As I made my way over to relieve Jimmy in the dog section, it occurred to me that we were now working together as a team at Barks & Beans. Instead of getting on my nerves as he initially had, Milo was proving to be quite multi-dimensional, even compassionate. And Jimmy was a real stand-up guy. Time flew by when I was talking with Charity and Kylie, too.

In short, our cafe was getting established and thriving.

I just hoped Leo Moreau wouldn't swoop in from nowhere and make a mess of everything.

25

THE LUNCH RUSH came and went, and by the time it was over, I was feeling back on an even keel after my rocky start to the day. I settled at a table with a chicken salad croissant—Charity's chicken salad was incredible—when my phone rang. Doctor Schneider was calling for some reason.

I quickly swallowed my bite of sandwich. "Hello?"

"Macy, I'm sorry to bother you at work. I really need to get down to your charming cafe soon—I pass it every morning on my way to Ivy Hill."

"Please do," I said. "How can I help you this afternoon?"

"First of all, I heard about the debacle with Jedi this morning. I'm so sorry. This reflects poorly on Ivy Hill. Alice would've fired him on the spot."

I glanced at the area where Bo had pinned Jedi to the floor. "Don't worry about it. It all worked out okay."

"Katie and I are discussing what to do about him. But in the meantime, I found something I thought you'd be interested in."

I took a sip of my hot mint tea, curious as to what he was talking about. "And what would that be?"

The doctor cleared his throat. "I recalled that you were interested in what had happened to Gerard's things, since you needed his dog's vet records. You know how I mentioned that Alice rented a storage building? I found the keys for it when I was cleaning her desk drawers. I'm happy to get the keys to you —I trust that you'll be able to find what you're looking for. You could just return them to me."

Although I'd already located Coal's vet and gotten the scoop on his records, it would be good to see if Gerard had saved more paperwork on his dog. Even more enticingly, he might've left a clue as to the meaning of Coal's mysterious metal tag.

Checking into a storage building had nothing to do with Ivy Hill, so Bo couldn't really be upset with me for looking into it.

Who was I kidding? He'd definitely be ticked if he knew what I was planning to do, but what he didn't know...

"Sure," I said. "Tell me the name of the storage place, and would you mind dropping the keys off at my house tonight? I live in back of the cafe, so it's on your way. Just open the back gate and come up to my door. I really appreciate this."

"Happy to help," the doctor said. "I'll drop by around six. Tonight's an early night for me."

I felt a little guilty about prying into Gerard's boxes, but if I turned up anything, it could only shine more light on things— possibly on his murderer. I convinced myself that Gerard would've wanted me to check things out.

Besides, Detective Hatcher had dismissively said the cops had searched Gerard's house right after the murder, and by now, they'd had plenty of time to check over the storage building, if they'd wanted to. I doubted they were concerned about the cryptic message on the metal dog tag, but I couldn't shake the hunch that it was directly connected to Gerard's murder and Coal's dognapping.

I was just gathering intel, that was all. There was no need to bother my brother to come along. I'd be in and out in no time.

After this, I'd stop worrying about what that tag meant. The cops had to be closing in on Gerard and Alice's murderer...or murderers...by now.

Didn't they?

Doc Schneider knocked on my door at 6:10. Coal gave a bellowing bark and charged forward, so I shoved him behind me before cracking the door to peek out.

"Hi," I said. "Sorry about the dog."

The doctor smiled. "He came with me easily enough after Gerard's death, but he's been through a lot since then, hasn't he?"

When Coal heard the doctor's voice, he poked his nose around me and sniffed. The doctor held out a hand and Coal inched toward him.

"He likes you," I said.

"I'm glad he's found a good home." The doctor held out a couple of keys dangling from a keychain emblazoned with 6A. I reached out and took it.

"It's at the Meadow Field storage facility," he said. "I found the paperwork for Alice's building rental—which reminds me, we're going to have to figure out what to do with all Gerard's stuff so we won't have to keep paying rental fees. Let me know if you see anything valuable in there that we can sell. Otherwise, we'll just do a huge yard sale or something."

"Will do," I said. "It's too bad he didn't have any close relatives who could take care of these things for you."

"Gerard was used to being alone, I think." He nodded at Coal. "That dog was probably his closest friend." Glancing at the sky, he asked, "Are you going over now? It's so overcast and it'll be dark soon. But I imagine the building has a light."

I shoved the keys in my jeans pocket. "Probably. I'll take a flashlight, too."

"I'd offer to go with you, but my wife and I are dining out with friends tonight." He glanced at Coal. "Maybe you should take your dog with you. He seems quite protective."

"He's not the easiest animal to transport, and I don't think I'll need backup." I tried to sound carefree. "I'm sure people go to those storage facilities at all hours. Besides, you have to have a key to get in."

The doctor nodded. "I've just been struggling to make sense of Alice's death, not to mention Gerard's. The police asked me some rather pointed questions, which led me to believe Alice and Gerard were involved in underhanded activities at Ivy Hill."

"Art fencing," I confirmed. "But the police already have a serious suspect, so I'm sure you and I are off the hook. Glen Rhodes has been taken into custody, from what I've heard."

"Glen?" The doctor paled and placed a hand to his chest. "Surely not Glen Rhodes?"

I nodded. "He was there in Alice's office—they found his prints on a glass. Maybe they uncovered some DNA linking him to her strangulation."

"Glen's company was one of our largest donors," he said.

"That's what I heard."

Doctor Schneider shook his head. "I'm afraid it's going to take a miracle to keep Ivy Hill afloat. We'll probably dismiss Jedi, then if we lose that company donation too..." His voice trailed off and he furrowed his bushy eyebrows.

"Didn't the oyster roast bring in some donations?" I asked.

He nodded. "I deposited those checks, but after looking over Alice's books, I'm afraid that money will only serve to get us caught up on the bills." He shot me a desperate look. "I guess we've been on rocky ground for a while. Alice kept it hidden from everyone."

"I'm sorry." I was at a loss for what to say.

He gave a curt nod and glanced at his watch. "Maybe I'll have to go back into private practice—a rather daunting thing at my age," he said. "But I'd better get going, or I'll be late for dinner. Take care of yourself. Just drop the key off when you're done with it."

"Thank you," I said, closing the door as he headed down the garden path. Coal gave a plaintive whine, and I patted his head. "What's up, boy? You remember the doctor? He's nice, huh?" I couldn't really believe Doc Schneider was so trusting with the entirety of Gerard's earthly possessions, but then again, it wasn't really his direct responsibility. Alice had taken that burden on herself, and now Alice was dead.

I shivered. It *was* getting dark fast, and it was chilly, too. I sprinted upstairs and chose a black turtleneck sweater, my black jeans, and black boots for my mission. Maybe I'd blend into the shadows if anyone *did* turn out to be lurking around the storage facility.

It was tempting to take Coal along, but I knew that was far more hassle than it was worth. I was going to be fine. The doctor was the only one who knew I was heading over to Meadow Field Storage tonight, and he was going out with his wife. I'd lock the building door once I got inside, so no one could burst in while I was going through things.

I fed Coal and walked him, then tucked him in with his blanket on his pillow. He gave me a reproachful stare, as if he knew what I was up to.

"I'm working tomorrow—early shift," I explained for

absolutely no reason. "I want to go through things before they unload Gerald's stuff. This is the best time to do it."

Coal yawned and gave me a doggie groan.

"Get some sleep," I commanded, grabbing my car keys and easing into my black coat. "I've got unfinished business to take care of." I whisked out the door, making sure to lock it behind me.

MEADOW FIELD STORAGE Facility turned out to be a well-lit area that was completely gated. I pulled up in front of the main gate, then took out my keys to try them in the lock. When I stepped closer, it was obvious someone had left the main gate unlocked, so I only had to push it open. I fingered the knife in my jeans pocket, just in case. It was probably normal for someone to be on the premises at this time of day, but it wouldn't hurt to be cautious. I drove in and parked, then walked around the long metal buildings until I found 6A.

The garage-style door was locked with a padlock that was bolted to the floor. I tried a couple of keys before finding the one that opened it. I rolled the metal door upward, then felt for an interior light switch and flipped it on.

As I slid the door back down, closing it behind me, I realized there was no way to lock the door from inside. This was probably a good thing for most people, so they didn't get stuck in the windowless room, but it wasn't so wonderful for me. I didn't want anyone surprising me while I was perusing Gerard's things.

I glanced around at the piled-up furniture that was covered with blankets. It seemed things had been stored willy-nilly. Had Alice hired movers to clear Gerard's house, or had she enlisted someone to help her with the gigantic chore? Whoever had unloaded things hadn't been very organized about it.

I found a tall, empty wooden bookshelf near the wall. After much heaving and shoving, I managed to position the heavy shelf so that it wedged against the ceiling, effectively blocking the door from sliding up. No one would be able to burst in on me with that in place.

I rummaged through several boxes and finally found one with manila file folders. I found one titled *Coal* and browsed through it, but it was the same information the vet had given me. Nothing about the cryptic numerical code on the tag.

I had another thought. What if Amber happened to be a woman? The police had probably checked Gerard's computer files and phone, but maybe that was before I'd given them the Amber tag.

I glanced around, my eyes landing on a bedside table. Surely Alice had cleaned that out before moving it...

I walked over and yanked the single drawer open. Alice hadn't even bothered to empty the drawer before packing it. If Gerard was anything like me or most people I knew, he might've kept more private things in his bedside table. I rooted through a jumble of books—inspirational quotes, Sudoko puzzles, and a worn dog training book.

My fingers closed around a thin gray book, which I slid out into the light. A journal, perhaps? As I opened it, I realized it was a planner for this year.

Had the police even noticed this?

I thumbed through the pages. Penciled-in names seemed to indicate his appointments with golf students. I tried to recall the day he'd died—it was a couple of days after our opening, because I remembered Charity talking about it. I flipped to September.

Gerard only had a few clients scheduled for that month.

Isabella Rhodes was one of them, but that wasn't a fact she'd ever tried to hide. In fact, she'd almost seemed proud of her rapport with her adored golf instructor.

I looked for other familiar names in the slots during the week he'd been killed. He'd written Alice's name at nine on a Monday night, but I was guessing that marked the conference call they'd had with Glen Rhodes and Leo Moreau.

Doctor Schneider was also on the list during the week before Gerard's death, but that lined up with what he'd told me about Gerard fearing for his life. Gerard had scheduled time to talk with the psychologist and request that he take Coal if anything happened to him.

My eyes landed on a name that was scheduled just two days before Gerard's death. I caught my breath and reread those three words, disbelieving.

Before I could reason why Gerard would've set up that meeting, I heard the absolute worst sound I could've imagined.

The door creaked as the back of it banged into the tall bookshelf. Someone was trying to get in.

Not a moment later, the door was rammed upward again—and this time it inched open a little. Whoever was out there was very determined.

I leapt under the dining room table, peeking around the tattered blanket that was draped over it. I slid my phone from my pocket. Should I call 9-1-1 or my brother?

Bo would probably get here faster.

I hesitated. If I spoke out loud on the phone, it would leave the intruder no doubt someone was in here. But if I only texted Bo, he might not notice it until morning.

I pressed the call button.

Thankfully, Bo picked up fast. "What's—"

"I'm stuck in a building and someone's trying to get in," I whispered.

"What? I couldn't hear—"

I spoke a bit louder as the ramming noises continued. "I'm in storage building 6A at the Meadow Field Storage place. Someone's trying to break in here." Things fell silent outside and I could see that the bottom of the door was now propped open several inches. They had likely heard me talking. "Come quick!" I hissed.

"On my way." Bo hung up.

It was a ten minute drive. I could be lying here dead by the time my brother showed up.

I pulled out my pocket knife, but it seemed miserably short-bladed. Crawling around slowly, I carefully reached into boxes, hoping to turn up some kind of makeshift weapon with a longer reach.

The back of the rolling door thudded against the bookshelf, and I watched in horror as the narrow shelf actually wobbled. My fingers wrapped around something long and cold in one box...a fireplace poker.

That would do.

I crouched back under the table, pulling the blanket down lower. Minutes passed as someone repeatedly thrust the loud door upward. How was no one else hearing all this racket?

But then things fell ominously silent for a couple of minutes. I froze in position. I was *not* impressed with the security of the Meadow Field Storage Facility.

Could someone be aiming a gun inside the building?

A strong, sudden heave pushed the bookshelf backward enough that I was sure someone could now slip under the opening. I held my breath, grasping the poker. I was ready to spring and attack the moment someone pulled the blanket up.

"Sis?"

Bo? It took me a minute to wrap my mind around the fact that it was my brother who'd just crawled into the room.

"Here!" I scrambled out from under the table, holding the poker at my side. "Did you see anyone?"

Bo rubbed at his arms, which must be sore from that powerful—and successful—break in. "No one. I scouted around the building first. They must've run."

I climbed over a couple of boxes to give him a hug. I was too shaken to even say thanks, but I knew he didn't expect it.

What he *would* expect, however, was an explanation.

Sure enough, that was the first thing he asked for. "Could you please tell me why you were rummaging around a storage building in the middle of the night? Who does this even belong to?"

"Gerard Fontaine. It was supposed to be a harmless expedition. Doctor Schneider—he's that psychologist I told you about—gave me the keys to this storage unit so I could find all Coal's records before they turn all Gerard's stuff over for a big yard sale." I gave Bo my most innocent look, as if to say, *Wouldn't you want me to have all my dog's records?*

Bo shook his head, unimpressed. "Forgive me if I miss my guess, but you weren't perhaps trying to find out more about that message on the metal dog tag while you were in here?"

"Maybe," I said. "But I wanted the records, too. Besides, the cops have already gone over this stuff. There didn't seem to be any danger in it." Even I had to admit how ridiculous I sounded, now that someone—most likely someone dangerous—had been doing their best to get at me in the storage unit.

Bo stood still, as if lost in thought. I realized he was wearing his plaid pajama pants and had thrown on a pair of Crocs. He really *had* arrived on the scene in record time.

"Okay." His tone was brisk. "Let's look around. Maybe Alice hid something here before she was killed, or maybe we'll find out why someone wanted that tag so much they stole your dog. How about you look through things and I'll guard the door?"

"With what?" I asked.

He unzipped his jacket and pointed to his shoulder holster, where his large Glock was sitting pretty. "Don't worry about it. Just get searching."

"You got it, bro." I pulled out my flashlight and started digging through boxes, trying to hide how elated I felt that Bo had come around to seeing what an opportunity this might be.

It was our chance to answer some pressing questions, and maybe—just maybe—to uncover a murderer in the process.

26

It was 11:41 and I'd gone through nearly everything in the building when I finally found something that seemed out of place. Gerard had stuffed a colorful child's copy of *Ali Baba and the Forty Thieves* into a box of books. That book didn't make sense if he didn't have any immediate family and no children of his own, unless it was a favorite relic of his childhood. I pulled it from the box and flipped through it, and a pamphlet from Ivy Hill fell out.

Snatching it up, I started examining it. Maybe Gerard had used the pamphlet as a bookmark, but that didn't make sense for such a short book. The pamphlet included a map of the Ivy Hill grounds, and one section looked a bit darker than the rest. I turned my flashlight beam on it. Just off the left side of the golf course in the wooded area, Gerard had drawn a rudimentary sketch of a tree with a split trunk.

"I think I have something," I said, holding the map out to Bo. "Check out the left edge of the golf course."

Bo held it up to the ceiling light. "Maybe he was just bored one day and started doodling."

"I think it means something. It's like he was marking that tree, you know?"

Bo nodded and yawned. "Possibly. We have to get to work early—let's call it a night for now. Bring it with you, and we can talk about it in the morning." He opened the door and ushered me toward it, flipping off the light before following me out. "Go ahead and lock up. I'll follow your car back to your place."

I pulled down the unit door and clicked its padlock shut. Once we'd both driven out the main gate, I pulled over in the parking area and Bo did, too. I walked back to the main gate, trying keys until I found the one that locked it behind us.

As I headed home, questions swirled in my head. Had some stalker followed me in through the unlocked main gate? Or was the person already on the premises when I arrived? Did they own a key to the main gate?

It was also possible that the attempted break-in at the storage unit had nothing to do with me. Someone could have been confused about their own unit number and gotten concerned, assuming someone had broken in. Or maybe someone planned to rob a random unit and they'd noticed 6A was unlocked.

Both options seemed unlikely, but they weren't outside the realm of possibility.

I pulled into my parking spot outside my house, and Bo eased his truck in behind me. He accompanied me up to my back porch and waited until I unlocked the door and stepped inside. Coal roused from his bed and thundered over to me.

"Get some sleep. We'll talk tomorrow." He sounded a little grouchy, but it was understandable given his run-in with Jedi this morning, not to mention my desperate call tonight.

I nodded. "Thanks again." Closing the door and locking it, I turned back to Coal, whose tired eyes were nonetheless expectantly fixed on me.

"Let me get you a treat," I said, extracting one from the canister for him. "You're a good boy."

He snatched it up and gobbled it, then wagged his massive tail.

"Time for bed now," I said, leading the way upstairs. I knew one thing for sure—I needed to check out that tree Gerard had marked. But would Bo agree to come along with me, even though it was venturing into Ivy Hill territory, though not so directly? Maybe we could sneak into the woods from the roadside somewhere...

I threw on my red reindeer pajamas—some of the only long-sleeved PJs I'd unpacked at this point—and snuggled under my covers. Tomorrow was a new day, as Scarlett O'Hara always said, and I was hoping it'd be less eventful than today.

My phone rang and woke me up at 5:35 in the morning. I groaned, but saw that it was Summer, so I picked up. "Hello?"

Summer was so congested I could hardly understand her. "I'm not going to be able to bring the dogs today. I'm sick."

"Aw, you sound miserable. I'm so sorry," I said. "I'll drop by and get them."

"Most of my staff is sick," she continued, barking out a not-so-muffled cough. "I'm closing the shelter for today."

"Oh," I said. "You want me to get the key and pick up the dogs?"

"No," she said firmly. "You'll get sick and this cold is miserable. Maybe it's even the flu—who knows?"

"Okay, well, thanks for calling. We'll manage just fine. Hope you get to feeling better."

She said goodbye and I rolled over to go back to sleep, but my thoughts were racing. People were going to come in, expecting to kick back and pet dogs today just like any other day at Barks & Beans. I couldn't let them down.

Coal stretched and yawned. I smiled.

"Thanks for volunteering," I said. "We might not have a lot of pups today, but we'll have one oversized dog who can illustrate just how successful shelter placements can be. You'll be my poster child, Coal."

I GAVE Coal a brushing and a good long garden walk before we headed over to the cafe. Bo was unloading a shipment in the back room, so I snagged a scone and went in to tidy the doggie room. Coal stayed close to me, excited about his new adventure, but still a bit apprehensive.

The hours raced by uneventfully, punctuated only with customers gasping over Coal's size and friendliness. Every time they asked how I'd gotten him, I was happy to recommend the shelter.

I was surprised when Dylan strode in just before lunchtime. I'd struggled with misgivings about the suave art gallery owner, but ever since my visit to storage building 6A, I had even more reason to distrust him. I'd found three words scrawled in Gerard's planner—a place he must've visited just two days before he was murdered. Those words were "The Discerning Palette."

Dylan's art gallery.

Had Dylan told the police about Gerard's visit to his gallery? I didn't think so. Which meant he was very actively hiding something.

Dylan picked up a coffee and a muffin before striding over to me. "Macy," he said, obviously happy to see me. He was about to step into the dog area when Coal sidled up beside me and sat down.

Dylan froze, his coffee and muffin clutched tight. "Is this—"

"My dog," I finished. "Dylan, meet Coal."

Dylan gave a stiff smile. "He's quite handsome."

Coal's mouth hung open and his teeth were on full display, even though he was merely panting a little.

Dylan was obviously uncomfortable. "Perhaps he doesn't want me getting near you?"

I remembered Dylan had said he was a cat person, and that couldn't be more evident. Although Coal's body language was hardly foreboding as he gave a slow wag of his tail, Dylan seemed cowed by the Dane's gigantic size.

I should have set him at ease, but I was irritated that Dylan hadn't been up front about *all* his run-ins with Gerard when I'd asked. "It's probably okay if you come in here, but I can just have a seat with you out there, if you'd rather?"

Dylan seemed to relax. "That'd be great."

I gave Coal a toy and washed my hands, then stepped into the cafe. We sat at a table where Coal could still keep an eye on me.

"I actually came here today with a purpose," Dylan said, offering me a bite of muffin.

I declined, since it was nearly time for my lunch break. "Really? And what's that?"

He grinned, which highlighted his strong cleft chin. How very Cary Grant. "Do you remember I mentioned we're doing an art gallery showing? It's coming up on Monday night, and I wanted to give you a personal invite. I think you'd enjoy it—didn't you say you're a Bierstadt fan? Of course, we don't have any of his paintings on show—I couldn't even fit one of his huge paintings in my gallery—but we'll be showing some Hudson

River School paintings with that same luminous quality." He took a sip of coffee and slid a flyer toward me.

My eyebrows rose as I looked at some of the paintings that would be featured. "That's some pretty impressive stuff you'll be showing."

"It helps to know people," he said. "Tell me you'll come?"

He wasn't hiding his interest in me, but there was no way I was going to trip blithely into some liar's arms. "Sure...I'll think about it," I hedged. "Hey, do you remember Gerard Fontaine, the golf instructor?"

Dylan's brow creased. "Yes. Why?"

I glanced over to the coffee bar, where Bo was serving a customer. He'd have my back if Dylan did anything stupid.

"Because I found his planner," I said candidly. "It showed that he'd visited your gallery a couple of days before he died, and I wondered why." I gave Dylan a sugary sweet smile.

He looked pensive for a brief moment, then swatted at the air. "Oh, I'd totally forgotten! He'd scheduled an appointment to get an estimate on his great grandma's vase. It certainly wasn't anything to write home about."

"What kind of vase was it?" I asked quickly, hoping to catch him off-guard.

He didn't hesitate to answer. "It was decorated with hand-painted antique roses, but it was hardly worth anything." He snapped his fingers. "Come to think of it, he did act a little weird. He kept glancing out my showroom windows, and he said he wanted to talk with me sometime about historical artifacts. Do you think he meant that Tiffany lamp or the rhino horn? Do you think he could've been involved with Alice?"

I knew he had been, and it probably didn't make a difference since Dylan was already connecting the dots. "Yes, I think they were involved in the same art fencing gig."

He gave a sage nod. "So it *was* fencing. I suspected that, given the pricey stuff Alice kept in her office."

I tried to act casual. "So, what have you been up to lately? Did you work late last night?" I didn't know if he ever worked late, but I wanted to see if he had an alibi for last night's attempted break in at storage unit 6A. Maybe he'd heard where Gerard's things were stored and he'd decided to visit Meadow Field. After all, if he managed to break into the unit, he'd instantly recognize any valuable artwork Gerard might have hidden there.

He stared at the deliberately scuffed wood tabletop as he took another sip of coffee. "No, I actually went to a restaurant. As you may have guessed, I eat out a lot. I'm afraid I'm not the best cook." As he raised his head, his eyes didn't quite meet mine.

"Where'd you go?" I felt like some kind of undercover detective with my line of questioning, but I needed to know if anyone could corroborate where he was last night. And he was acting shifty, after all.

This time, however, he held my gaze. "Over to that Italian place off 219. I had spaghetti and meatballs. They have the best garlic bread there. Why do you ask?"

I sighed a bit too loudly and tried to mask it with a yawn. "Just curious. I'm sorry, I was up late last night and I'm not the best company today." I hoped he wouldn't push for further explanation. Obviously, I was barking up the wrong tree with Dylan. After pushing my chair back, I stood. "I'll let you finish your food and I'll go back to my dog, who seems to be pining away for me."

That much was true—Coal's eyes hadn't wavered from following my every move since I'd walked into the cafe section, and he was starting to whine intermittently.

Dylan stood and gave my arm an awkward pat. It was clear

he sensed I was uncomfortable chatting with him. "Okay, well, please do drop by the show, if you can."

I noticed he'd downgraded the art show from a possible date to a "please drop by" type of thing on my account, but I didn't really care that I was coming off as chilly. I couldn't trust a man who wouldn't look me in the eyes and who'd conveniently forgotten that a murder victim had visited his gallery a couple days before he died, no matter how innocuous that visit had been.

27

Bo STAYED BUSY ALL DAY, and I knew when he was like that, it was better to steer clear. A large part of his troubled mood probably stemmed from our late-night storage building adventure, which meant he didn't want me bringing up the possibility that we head to Ivy Hill to search for the split-trunk tree Gerard had drawn on the map.

I really should let the whole thing drop, but I couldn't. Gerard had hidden that pamphlet, probably hoping someone would follow up on it, and it was likely a clue to the tag he'd hidden on Coal.

Besides, I'd told the doctor I'd drop the storage building keys off sometime, although I'd actually planned to pop them in the mail so I wouldn't have to return to Ivy Hill.

I wished I could ask Summer to come along with me, but she was obviously miserable with her cold. It'd be handy if I had more friends I could count on around here. Our employees would inevitably tell Bo what I was up to, and Dylan was hardly a trustworthy pick.

Still, there was a way I could avoid going out in the open on the Ivy Hill center grounds. I called Doc Schneider and asked him to pick the keys up on his way home, if he didn't mind. I told him I'd leave them just inside my back gate in a little basket.

In the meantime, I started planning a stealth invasion of the woods near the golf course. I pulled up the satellite images on my Maps app to see where the wooded area started and ended. It looked like my hunch was right—I could park alongside the road and hike into the woods. So I'd never *technically* be in the main area of Ivy Hill—shoot, I might not even be on their property.

I was fairly certain there wasn't any type of hunting season going on, but just in case, I'd wear a blaze orange hat.

I couldn't imagine the new golf instructor would pay much attention to some stranger wandering the edge of the golf course, if he even caught sight of me. If Gerard had been really serious about hiding something, surely he would've picked a tree that wasn't very obvious from the golf course.

I gave Bo another hug at the end of the work day. His eyes were lackluster and it was clear he was pooped. "Why don't you just get take-out and hit the sack?" I asked him. "I'm going to give myself a spa night at home—you know, nails, face mask, all that."

I felt bad lying to Bo, but I knew I couldn't loop him in on this mission. No one knew about Gerard's map but us, and I was a natural in the woods, so I was confident I could get in and out with no interference.

"Okay," Bo said, glancing at Coal, who had plopped down by my feet. "Your dog did great today, sis. I had so many customers gushing about how polite he was."

"Good publicity for the shelter *and* for Barks & Beans," I said. "Coal's been a real blessing, in more ways than one."

Bo scratched behind Coal's tall ears. "I'd have to agree. Hey, grab some fresh Guatemalan beans from the back—that stuff'll wake you up in the morning."

"I will. Thanks!"

I went to the back room and filled a paper bag with the glossy black beans. The smell was utterly intoxicating, so I decided to brew myself a cup when I got home. Instead of walking outside, I told Bo goodnight and went through the connecting door, straight into my house. Coal started frisking around, chewing at various toys, then digging into his food dish.

"You did great today, boy," I said. I hated to leave him alone again tonight, but I'd be an idiot not to follow up on this final clue Gerard had left behind. Besides, it might mean nothing—it could be a tree he'd carved with his initials, for all I knew. If I did find something of interest, I'd turn it right over to the police.

I tried to convince myself that whoever had attempted breaking into unit 6A hadn't been targeting me personally. It was probably just a fluke.

Besides, Alice's killer had already been arrested, and it was possible he'd killed Gerard, too. Someone wealthy like Glen Rhodes would've believed he couldn't be caught—though it was a supremely stupid move to leave his drinking glass on Alice's desk the night she was murdered. Still, I figured killers did stupid things in the heat of the moment. Who could say if Alice's murder was premeditated or not—or what benefit it was to Glen—but those were the kinds of things the police could figure out.

I was just following up on something I found in a dead man's paraphernalia, that's all.

Wanting to get over to the woods before it was completely dark, I bolted down another cup of coffee, practically inhaled half a ham sandwich, and dressed in warm clothes topped off with my blaze orange hat.

I loaded up a flashlight and a shovel, just in case I needed to dig around the spot Gerard had marked. After telling Coal goodbye and flipping on the TV for him, I locked up and deposited the doctor's storage building keys in a decorative grapevine basket just inside the gate.

I glanced down the street to make sure Bo hadn't gone out for a run, but saw no one. I slipped into my car and edged out into the street.

Using Maps, I found what looked to be a good entry point to get into the woods. I pulled off the road into a little turnaround area. After grabbing my supplies, I locked up the car and hiked into the trees.

At this point in October, many leaves still clung to limbs and the underbrush was still green, so I had a little cover. I inhaled deeply, taking in the earthy smells of the woods. There was nothing more relaxing to me than walking in the woods— not even the beach, which was my brother's happy place. No, I'd rather have both feet on the ground than feel them getting sucked in with ocean water where fish pooped, sharks lurked, and currents could catch and kill you.

Come to think of it, maybe I had a phobia of bodies of water because our parents had drowned. I should probably talk that out with Doc Schneider sometime, if it was ever safe to return to Ivy Hill. Or maybe he'd make a house call. Did psychologists ever do that? It probably wasn't recommended.

My mind stopped its random wandering when I caught sight of a tree that most certainly was the exact one Gerard had sketched. I'd forgotten to bring his map, but I remembered the drawing well. The tree he'd sketched was leaning on one side, just like the one in front of me, and it had a defined split trunk.

I hurried closer and turned on my phone flashlight as I circled the tree, looking carefully around the base of the trunk. The sun hadn't set yet, but I had to look closely in the rapidly fading daylight. Gerard hadn't carved anything into it, however, and there were no visible hollows on the tree.

Moving the beam of my light upward, I examined the niche between the conjoined trunks, but that appeared to be empty. Using my pocket knife, I dug into the leafy compost in the niche area, but it was hardly thick enough to hide anything.

That left one option—Gerard must've buried something here.

I looked past the tree to see how visible I was to anyone on the golf course. I was several car's lengths away from where the green started, and there was no one in sight on the course. It was probably closing soon, if not closed already, since the sun had started to set.

The ground wasn't too hard, so I shoved my phone into my back pocket, grabbed the shovel I'd dropped on the ground, and began to plunge it into the dirt. I moved in a loose circle around the tree. I didn't want to tear up the roots or make it obvious I'd been here, so I didn't dig shovelfuls out of the ground. I merely felt for a jolt that would inevitably happen if I struck something Gerard had buried.

I'd worked my way in toward the trunk when my shovel actually hit something hard. I pulled it out and angled the blade a bit to the right before pushing it into the ground with my foot. It hit something again.

Now I started digging in earnest, since the shadows were starting to swallow up the woods. After several minutes of coffee-fueled digging, I uncovered what had been buried.

It was a square metal box about the height of Bo's espresso maker. I pried it out with the shovel. There was no lock on it, so I used my knife to push into the seam where the lid met the body of the box. After much finagling, I was able to pull the top off.

Inside, there was a metal lockbox with some kind of

electronic code. Gerard had wisely used the airtight outer box to protect the electronic safebox inside.

Should I close it up and bury the box again, then try to explain its location to the cops? Or should I just heft it back to my car and drop it off directly to the police?

It was getting dark so fast, I decided it would be best to get it back to my car, then drive it to the police station tomorrow morning. I could hardly see where to dig at this point.

I took off my old, oversized coat and set the surprisingly lightweight box in the middle of it, then zipped the coat around it. I could only carry so much with me, so I propped my shovel against another tree, planning to retrieve it later. I needed to focus on getting the box to my car. Dragging it seemed a good option, so holding onto the hood of the coat with both hands, I tugged at the makeshift sled. Thankfully, the coat slid along relatively easily as I retraced my steps to my car.

I was pretty worn out by the time I unlocked my trunk and hefted the box inside. No one was in sight on the darkened back road, and I was grateful. I'd have to come up with some crazy night hunting story if someone saw me...and it might not even be hunting season.

On the way home, I marveled at the way things had gone off without a hitch. Surely there'd be something valuable inside the safebox Gerard had so carefully hidden—something the cops would definitely want to see.

Still, I didn't want to call them tonight. Since the police were staying in contact with Bo, they'd likely let him know of my find, which would in turn cut into yet another night of sleep for him. Although I had an uneasy feeling about making off with someone else's property, I knew it was groundless, because Glen was in jail right now. I'd just sit on the box until tomorrow.

I felt a stab of worry. What if Moreau was somehow

involved with this? What if Gerard had hidden something to keep it from his smuggler boss?

I turned on the heat to take out the chill in the car. Moreau was far away on some distant private island, Bo had said. Even if he had someone else in Ivy Hill keeping an eye on things—someone like Jedi or Katie—there had been no one around to see my secret dig.

I pulled into my parking space and contemplated popping the trunk, but decided to leave the safe in the car overnight. My arms were already tired from hauling the box from the woods.

Jogging up to my back door, I unlocked it and went inside. Coal's head was angled and he was actually watching a car chase on TV, which cracked me up. I was secretly proud I'd wound up with such an intelligent dog.

He got up and danced around me, and I realized he needed to get outside to relieve himself. I opened the door and let him run out into the fenced area while I scrounged around my kitchen for something to eat. I was famished after my secret mission, and adrenaline still coursed through my system. I dumped salsa into a bowl and grabbed a bag of chips, settling back into the couch to search for a show I wanted to watch. Suddenly, Coal's yowling barks reverberated through the house.

What on earth was going on? The dog rarely barked, but now he was full-on bellowing at something. I rushed out, certain he was going to wake the older neighbors and get me reported for breaking the noise ordinance.

He stood, stock still, his head erect and pointing toward the gate. I eased over that way, trying to see if he'd spotted someone trying to break in.

The streetlight illuminated a woman with a thermal head wrap and tennis shoes. She was standing on the sidewalk and stretching her legs. Catching a glimpse of my movement, she turned and we recognized each other. It was Isabella Rhodes, apparently taking an evening jog in town.

She gave me a brief wave and pulled earbuds from her ears, which explained why Coal's howling hadn't gotten to her yet. I placed a quieting hand on Coal's head and he stopped barking. However, he continued to emit a series of whiny groans as I walked over to the gate, as if to say that no one had the right to stop on the street outside *his* fence.

Isabella jogged closer. "I'm so sorry—I didn't realize your dog was barking. I crank really loud music for my jogs."

"I didn't realize you jogged in town," I said.

She shrugged. "I usually don't. I have a treadmill at home, but tonight I just needed to get *out*, you know? Mary Anne told me I needed to burn off some of my anxiety, and she was right. I feel better already."

I didn't see any need to beat around the bush. "I heard about your husband," I said. "I'm sure that was such a shock for you."

Her eyes were dark as she looked at me. "Yeah. Honestly, I've been a mess. I wish we'd never gone to that oyster roast."

I figured the oyster roast itself wasn't the catalyst for Glen's homicidal behavior, but it had to be unnerving for Isabella to realize she'd been married to someone who could murder in cold blood. On top of that, her upstanding husband had been involved in an art fencing ring.

The Rhodes' reputation was going to be tarnished in town from here on out. I looked at Isabella with her brand-name exercise gear and fancy headband. Would she have to go to work if Glen's company went under?

She pulled out a blingy cell phone. "I'm going to call my butler and have him pick me up," she said. "I didn't plan on jogging this long, but it felt so good to breathe the fall air and clear my head. I kind of got turned around and wound up in your part of the neighborhood."

"I understand." I felt a wave of sympathy for the real housewife of Lewisburg. "You want to come in and have something to drink while you wait? You probably shouldn't be jogging, now it's gotten so dark out."

She blinked. "Really? You're asking me in for a visit?" She put a manicured hand on my arm. "You're a real sweetie, Macy! Sure, I'd love to—maybe just a glass of water?"

I swung the gate open and Isabella stepped inside. Coal's groans ratcheted up to near-barks.

I shushed him as he started sniffing at Isabella. "Quiet. Come on with me," I said, pulling at his collar so he'd walk alongside me. I led the way to the back door and let Coal inside, then turned. "There are a couple of uneven steps there," I warned Isabella.

"I know. I saw them." she said, her voice unnaturally smug.

What was that all about? Was she making a jab at how old my house was? How rude.

I reached out to push open the screen door, but a hand yanked mine back. "Not so fast, coffee princess," Isabella said darkly. "You see, I saw those steps the last time I was here...when I came and stole your precious *dog*."

28

THE STREETLIGHT barely penetrated the darkness of my back garden, and I couldn't see Isabella's face clearly. Was she seriously telling me she'd stolen my dog? Isabella High Heels Rhodes?

"What are you talking about?" I asked, yanking my arm free of her hand.

The moment I broke free, something cold and hard nuzzled into my back. It was just the right size to be the barrel of a handgun, and I had no doubt it was.

Isabella had a gun.

"Who even *are* you?" I asked, my shock making me brash.

She chuckled. "I'd love to stay and chat—you know, since we're *friends* and all—but I'll keep it short. And don't make any sudden moves, because I have a nine millimeter aimed at you. Shut the back door, nice and slowly."

As I pulled the wooden door shut, I could see Coal turning in a circle, fluffing his pillow. I wished I hadn't shushed him so vigorously and shut down his guarding instinct for the evening.

I turned back toward Isabella and she took a step closer,

pressing the nose of the gun into my stomach. "My husband thought I didn't know about his secret fencing ring. He must've assumed I was a mindless idiot. But I listened in on his calls and had him followed. I figured out he was working with Gerard and Alice, then I realized they were running artwork through Ivy Hill. It wasn't hard for me to pump Gerard for information—after all, the man fell for me, hard. I talked to him one day and he told me about a big art score he'd stumbled into."

"What, something like a rhino horn? Or maybe a Tiffany lamp?" I asked, anger and more than a little curiosity getting the best of me.

"Much bigger. See, I taught history at high school—in particular, the World War Two era. So when Gerard was bragging about intercepting some famous Nazi loot, I feigned ignorance and teased him to tell me what it was."

I thought about whipping around and rushing into my not-quite-shut back door, but there was no way I'd be able to take one step without getting shot. I had to assume that Isabella, clueless as she'd seemed up until now, knew exactly what she was doing with a gun.

I guessed the best idea was to keep her talking, especially since she was proud of how she'd played both her husband and Gerard.

"So, what was it? Something worth killing for, I assume? Because you did kill Gerard and Alice, right?"

Her voice became smooth as honey. "It was worth killing for, yes. Gerard told me he'd gotten his hands on part of a panel from the Amber Room."

I knew exactly what she was talking about. In one of my art classes, we'd learned how the Nazis had dismantled a Russian room that had been lined in real amber. The treasures from that room would be worth hundreds of millions.

"So he told you where it was?" I asked, hoping to keep her talking so I could formulate an escape plan.

"Not really. He made some kind of joke about how his dog knew the secret, but no one else did. Next thing you know, he said he was going to tell Alice about it—he'd decided to donate the money from it to Ivy Hill so they could build an indoor pool and start up drug rehab classes. *Donate* it! Can you imagine? I had to stop him."

"So you met up with him when no one was around and bashed him on the head with a golf club?" I asked, wishing I could sit down. My legs were starting to cramp from standing so still. But I knew better than to shift Isabella's train of thought to anything to do with me.

"It was easy enough," she said. "And once he was dead, I went through his house—he'd given me the key, of course. I looked everywhere, but I couldn't find the panel. So I bought a big dog crate, then headed back the next day, planning to take his dog. But when I showed up, that interfering Doctor Schneider had already taken him to the shelter."

"So you had to steal him from me, because you realized maybe Gerard had hidden something on his dog?"

"Right. Besides, I'd decided to pull Alice into the loop at that point. I lured her in by telling her I knew about the fencing, but I promised to give her a big cut of the amber panel if she helped me find it." She laughed. "Alice didn't like dogs, but she agreed to help me snatch Coal one day when you were out. We wrangled him up to the attic at Ivy Hill— you actually heard him barking that night, remember? I realized you wouldn't give up on looking for him in the main building, so Alice and I moved him over to that abandoned shed. We also took him to an out-of-town vet to get him X-rayed. Since we didn't know how big the amber piece was, we thought it was possible that Gerard had surgically implanted a smaller piece into the dog, but he hadn't, of course."

I leaned against the porch railing, forcing my knees not to give out. She was going to kill me, right here on the porch of my own home.

Sensing my unrest, Isabella barked, "Sit down on the step!"

I slowly sank into a seated position. "Isn't your butler coming soon?"

Her white teeth glinted as she answered. "I never called him. See, I came here following you. In my own car. Actually, I've followed you since you pulled out of the woods over by Ivy Hill." She crouched down, the gun catching the light from the street as she waved it near my face. "So if you know what's good for you, you'll tell me what you know about Gerard's treasure. Did you find it?" Her voice took on an edge. "If not in the woods, then maybe in the storage unit?"

So *she* was the one who'd tried to break in there, too. "I didn't find anything," I lied. "Maybe Alice did?"

She leaned closer. "Alice served her purpose, but then she started getting cold feet. She said she was going to get out of art fencing altogether, and that she didn't want the 'blood money' from Gerard's amber piece to fund Ivy Hill anyway. That Tiffany lamp was going to be the last thing she moved through the place. She had an attack of conscience, I guess."

"So you got rid of her before she could confess?"

"Of course, and I decided to frame Glen in the process. Really, it was the perfect setup. I took Glen's glass, but I kept my sleeves pulled over my fingers so only his prints showed up on it."

I sighed. "That's pretty smart. But you seriously strangled Alice all by yourself?" I was getting shaky as I realized she wouldn't keep talking for long. If she got more demanding, I'd have no choice but to give up Gerard's metal box to save my life.

"Piece of cake," she said. "I told Alice she had something on the back of her shirt, then I went around to take it off...and pulled her scarf tight around her neck. I grabbed the Tiffany lamp on my way out—I went down the fire escape stairs out back, so no one saw me. Then I stashed the lamp in the trunk of my car and went back and joined the party. Glen had gone to use the bathroom, which gave me the perfect opportunity to draw attention to the fact that he wasn't with the crowd when Alice was killed."

She was cold, all right. Cold enough to kill two people and frame her husband for it. She was definitely going to kill me if I didn't cooperate.

"Enough talking," she said abruptly. "You've been distracting me, haven't you? Getting me to toot my own horn?" She gave a callous laugh. "You know I can't let you live now, right? I basically confessed everything to you."

"I won't tell anyone, I swear." My stupid voice wavered, betraying me.

"You lie!" She was practically shouting. I wished any of my neighbors had left their windows open, but given the low temps, everyone was probably running their heat.

Shoving me aside, she sat down right next to me on the step. She moved the gun barrel up to my head and pressed it against my temple.

My breathing had gotten shallow, and I was fairly certain I was going to pass out. On the bright side, passing out could only ease the process of getting shot to death.

"Tell me where the amber is," she demanded.

"Okay," I said, unwilling to hedge any longer. "It's in the trunk of my car. In a metal box Gerard had buried in the woods."

"How did you know where it was? You're not lying to me, are you?" The cold gun barrel poked against my skin and I tried to take a deep breath.

"I tracked it down—took some work," I said.

She stood and stretched out her empty hand. "You know what? I don't want the whole story on your little treasure hunt. Just give me your car keys."

The hand that held the gun had relaxed at her side. Was she going to shoot me the moment I handed over the keys? Or would she get the metal box first?

"Sure," I said, slowly standing as I reached into my pocket. "You have to insert the key in the trunk lock—it's an older car."

She took the keys and jangled them in her hand. "Thanks for being so helpful. Now I'm going to have to ask you to come along with me."

"Okay," I said, counting on the darkness to hide me as I backed into the doorbell.

The moment it rang, Coal set off into a furious spree of barking. I jumped off the porch and raced into the dark garden, where I squeezed behind the boxwood hedge.

"Get back here *now!*" Isabella's low shout dripped venom.

That shout was Isabella's biggest mistake to date. She had her back turned to my house as she searched for me, but I was staring right at the back porch. Light from the house grew brighter as the wooden door was nudged open. The next thing I knew, the screen door was rammed backward as Coal came streaking out of the house, his deep barks indicating that he'd charged out at top speed. He launched himself at Isabella's back.

"What—" she shouted, but her voice was immediately muffled as she thudded to the ground.

The back gate burst open and I could see a man's outline.

"Macy!" Bo shouted over the sound of Coal's increasingly frantic howls. I could see he was holding his gun.

I scrambled out from my hiding place, shouting at Bo as I ran toward him. "I'm here! Coal's tackled a woman with a gun!"

Bo leaned in toward my ear. "Sneak around behind me and turn on the porch light. I'll deal with her."

By now, Isabella was yelping, as if in pain. "Get your brute dog off me! I can't move! I'll kill you!"

I managed to reach inside the door and flip the light on. Bo was standing over Isabella, his gun pointed at her chest. "Take her gun!" he shouted. "I've kicked it toward you!"

I hurried over to grab the weapon, then focused on the scene that was playing out in front of me.

Coal had literally stretched out on top of Isabella's chest, effectively pinning her entire upper half to the ground. He'd planted his hind end right up by her face, which seemed a fitting touch.

"We've got her," Bo said. "Call the cops."

"You got it, bro." I shakily pulled out my phone, dialed 9-1-1, and asked that Detective Hatcher be notified immediately of an armed break-in at my place. Was I ever going to have a story to tell him.

29

THE NEXT DAY dawned with a cloudless, deep blue sky, almost like it was celebrating our victory from the night before. Isabella was now in jail where she belonged. I rolled out of bed and slid into my slippers. Coal roused from his pillow and padded over to me.

"Good dog. *Good* dog," I repeated. I'd have to be careful not to spoil him with treats after his incredible act of bravery last night.

It was my day off, and I knew what to do with it. I was going to whip up a pot of homemade chicken noodle soup—one of the few recipes I excelled at—and drop some by Summer's place. When she'd called to let me know one of her employees would be bringing the dogs to the cafe for Jimmy this morning, she'd still sounded awful. Besides, I wanted to tell her what really happened to Gerard and Alice.

Padding downstairs, I ground the Guatemalan beans and brewed a couple of cups with my French press. After the third sip, some part of my brain finally woke up and I realized that I'd totally forgotten to hand over Gerard's metal box to Detective

Hatcher last night. Things had been chaotic, with Coal barking and Isabella ranting about false arrest and me trying to explain what had really happened.

I was just about to dial Detective Hatcher when my doorbell rang. Coal gave a huge bark and I told him to be quiet. I cracked the door and looked out, blinded by the sunshine that was hitting the back porch.

"Macy Hatfield?" a deep voice asked.

I bristled. Coal trotted over to my side, as if picking up on my unease. I could make out dark hair and a very tall male form, but I could hardly see the man's face and eyes.

"I'm FBI agent Titan McCoy," the man said, flashing a badge at me. "We've been looking into the dealings at Ivy Hill, and Detective Hatcher recommended I follow up with you after the events of last night."

"You don't say." I kept the door nearly shut. I knew I sounded skeptical, but I had good reason to after everything that had happened. "Maybe Detective Hatcher should've called to let me know you were coming."

The dark-haired man chuckled and leaned in a little. I could suddenly make out every detail of his face. He was probably in his early forties, with friendly but wary eyes. He was clean shaven, but had that kind of five o'clock shadow that made it evident his beard grew in fast. He wore jeans and a sweater, not the suit I'd imagined FBI agents wore.

"You're right; he should have. Macy, I've talked with your brother, Bo, if that helps put your mind at ease. I realize you've been through a lot these past few weeks." He glanced down at Coal, who had pushed his head out to stare at the agent. "I understand someone dognapped your beautiful dog here, as well. I'm glad you got him back." He offered me a smile that was serious, yet so earnest it was endearing.

I took one more look at his badge for good measure, then,

feeling fairly confident that Coal wouldn't try to attack the man, I opened the door wide and gestured to my couch. "Yes. Let me introduce you to my dog, Coal. You can come on in."

Titan took a step inside, and surprisingly, Coal politely moved out of his way.

I tried to be hospitable, even though I was feeling anything but after last night. "Please have a seat. Would you like a cup of coffee?"

"I'd love one." He strode to the couch, not even hesitating as Coal picked up pace alongside him, sniffing at his pants. "The coffee smells amazing."

I heated it a little in the microwave and added the cream he asked for. Then I joined him in the living room, where Coal had settled down—right on top of the man's leather shoes.

I handed him his mug. "It would seem my dog likes you. So...is your name actually Titan, or is that a code name?"

He grinned. "I wondered when that question was coming, because it always does. Let's just say my mom was *deeply* enthralled with Greek mythology. I'm just thankful she didn't wind up naming me Poseidon or Helios or something."

"Or Zeus," I said. He seemed a little less intimidating now that we were both sitting and he wasn't towering over me. In fact, I was surprised at how easily I was conversing with him. "Although Zeus sounds more like a dog's name. Do you remember Zeus and Apollo on *Magnum, P.I.?*

"They were Dobermans, right? I loved that show." He pulled out a small notebook before taking a sip of his coffee. "Wow, this is so rich."

"My brother knows a lot about coffee beans and where to buy the best ones," I said. "But you probably already knew that."

Titan nodded. "Bo and I have worked together in the past. Your brother's a natural in the field." It was a little unsettling to realize that this man had been part of my brother's DEA world when I had not.

Titan took a longer drink before clearing his throat. "Okay, so I've read over your statement from last night—you said Isabella confessed to the murders of Gerard Fontaine and Alice Stevenson. Isabella attempted to frame her husband, Glen, for Alice's murder. I've been updated on the art treasures Alice fenced through Ivy Hill, as well. However, we are still interested in one particular treasure that's still unaccounted for. I wondered if you could shine some light on that?"

"You're talking about the piece of the Amber room," I said. "Sure I'll share about it, and I'll do you one better. I dug up a metal box Gerard Fontaine buried on the grounds at Ivy Hill. Inside, there's an electronic safebox." My excitement was building as I realized I might actually get to *see* the historic panel. "I'm pretty sure I know the code that will open it. Gerard had some numbers engraved on a metal dog tag he hid on Coal, and I handed the tag over to the police. It started with the word *Amber*."

Titan nodded and flipped through his notebook. "Yes, I have the numbers here. But you said you have the box?"

I had a sudden flood of misgiving. I'd watched too many detective shows where someone showed up, posing as an FBI agent, and took stolen goods from some naive, trusting citizen.

"Could I see your badge one more time?" I asked.

Titan smiled and flipped open his black badge wallet. It had his photo card and signature on one side, and the iconic gold FBI badge on the other.

It looked convincing, but those things could be forged, I imagined. "Uh...could you hang on a minute?" I asked. "I need to use the bathroom."

"Sure." His slow smile indicated that he might know exactly

what I was up to. I didn't care. I couldn't afford to trust the wrong person, like I'd done so many times in the past.

I raced upstairs, trusting that Coal would stay in place on Titan's feet. I shut my bedroom door and gave Bo a call. "There's someone here named Titan McCoy, and he says he knows you. Is that right? Is he really FBI?"

"Titan? Oh, yeah, he's a great guy. He's over at your place now?"

"Yes. I just needed to make sure—"

"I'll run right over. I'm on break now anyway, and I'd like to see Big T."

I snickered as I hung up. So Titan was "Big T," was he?

I smoothed my wayward hair as I descended the stairs. "I'm so sorry. I just needed to take a little breather. It's all been so much," I said.

"You called your brother, didn't you?" he asked, his lips quirking into another grin.

I dropped into a chair. "You can't just trust anyone these days." I couldn't resist a final jab. "Especially someone with the last name of *McCoy*. I'm a Hatfield by blood, you know?"

Titan heaved a longsuffering sigh. "Really? And here I thought your brother had beaten that little pun into the ground. Yes, Hatfields *can* work with McCoys, I assure you."

There was a rap on the interior connecting door and the lock turned. Bo charged in, directly toward the living room. Titan jumped to his feet—somehow managing to leave Coal in place—and greeted Bo with a vigorous, back-patting man hug.

The men started rehashing stories of missions that were both terrifying and hilarious. I found myself feeling exceptionally grateful that my brother had lived long enough to become the mild-mannered barista and coffee shop owner he was today.

My stomach had just started growling for some breakfast

when Titan turned back to me. "So, you said you have the metal box, Macy?"

I nodded and rose, setting my empty coffee cup on an end table. "Bo, could you help me get it from the trunk?"

I opened the back door and paused to glance around the garden, where the dirt showed signs of the scuffle we'd had last night. "I can't believe she showed up at my house," I said finally.

Bo draped a comforting arm around my shoulders, his red hair shining copper in the sunlight. "She was a desperate woman, Macy. She was willing to set her own husband up for a life prison sentence. I heard Glen Rhodes was released on bail today."

I found myself hoping Glen would continue to donate to Ivy Hill, so Doctor Schneider could keep up his work there. Maybe he and Katie would find a way to keep the place financially viable.

I opened the trunk and Bo took the metal box out as if it weighed nothing. We walked it back into the house and set it on the kitchen counter. Titan had the string of numbers from the metal tag at the ready, and he punched them in on the safebox keypad.

The thing whirred and unlocked. I held my breath as Titan opened the lid.

A warmly-hued slab the size of a large coffee bag practically glowed in the bottom of the safe. Its honey colors seemed lit from within and ornate patterns were inlaid in it. I knew from art history class that there was gold leaf backing the panel.

We all stared at it, spellbound.

"What'll happen to it?" I finally asked.

"We'll be working with international agencies to determine if it's original to the Amber Room, then we'll start tracking where it came from."

"Exactly," Bo said. "How did Gerard get his hands on it?"

"You can guess *how*." Titan shot Bo a dark look. "We're looking for the where."

"You mean Moreau? You think he knew about this?" Bo asked.

Titan nodded. "We suspect Fontaine intercepted an art shipment he was supposed to deliver. He did some searching on the internet—we hacked into his computer—and he realized it was a real panel from the Amber Room. We think he made the very unwise choice of double-crossing Moreau. He probably lied and told Moreau he never got that shipment."

I offered both men a granola bar, and when they refused, I ate a few bites myself to quell my growling stomach. "I have a theory—I think Gerard told Alice about what he'd done. They weren't getting along right before he died. He could've admitted he'd lied to Moreau. I'm betting Alice realized what a deadly stupid mistake Gerard had made."

"Meanwhile, Isabella was circling, and she turned out to be the more immediate threat," Titan said. "We'll be grilling her and Glen, to see what they know about Moreau."

Bo cracked his knuckles. "It always comes back to Moreau, doesn't it? Even in my hometown. I can't get away from that man."

Titan slapped Bo's back. "Cheer up. We're on the case. You know I'm not going to let anything slide. I'll keep you posted with anything I find, and you know we're watching Leo. He's not going to sneak up on you, I promise."

As Titan began to close the safebox lid, I put my hand over his large one. "Wait—could I just touch it?"

He looked thoughtful.

"I *was* the one who found the map and had to hike out into the woods to dig it up," I said.

"You went out and did what?" Bo turned a fierce gaze on me.

Apparently my brother hadn't heard the whole story yet.

Titan opened the box wider. "Okay, but just one finger. I'll explain that you touched it in my presence. They'll definitely be dusting it for prints."

Slowly and near-reverently, I used my pinkie to reach into the box and touch the smooth, cool piece of amber. This discovery would go down in history, and I had been the one to make sure the panel wasn't hidden forever in a leaf-strewn grave.

"You're practically glowing, too," Titan said. "I think your hair's the exact same color as that amber, Macy."

Bo shot Titan a big brotherly look, and the FBI agent immediately turned brusque. "I'm going to load it up now. Thanks so much for finding this and handing it over." He closed both lids and turned to Bo. "Good to see you, man. I'll be in touch."

As agent Titan McCoy strode out my doorway—not an easy feat, given that Coal had taken to sniffing his shoes—I found myself hoping he'd show up in Lewisburg again someday.

But only if his visit had nothing whatsoever to do with tracking Leo Moreau.

30

ONCE THE CHICKEN soup was made and I was sure I'd put enough salt in it (my chronic soup failing), I called Summer to see where she lived. Turned out, she rented an apartment over an older couple's garage.

When I knocked on her door, soup and homemade bread in hand, she seemed delighted to see me.

"I've just cleaned the entire place with Pine-Sol," she said. "Stay well away from me and you shouldn't get this nasty bug."

"Thanks," I said, placing the soup and bread on the cabinet. I was surprised when a fluffy gray cat slunk up by my side. "You have a cat?"

She nodded. "Three cats, to be exact, and one kitten I'm fostering for a while. Didn't you realize I'm a cat person?"

"I guess I assumed you were into dogs, like me." I sat on an overstuffed chair, where the gray cat jumped onto my lap and began lightly kneading at my jeans.

"Ella, knock that off," Summer commanded. "I'm okay with dogs—I mean they don't scare me, but cats are a lot more manageable. In fact, I was thinking your brother might like a cat...maybe even the kitten I'm taking care of." She gave a quirky little whistle, and the kitten came running. It was a beautiful long-haired calico.

Summer swept it up and cradled it close. "I haven't named her yet, but she potty trained fast. She doesn't miss the litterbox and actually comes when I call her. She can be a little frisky, but that's normal for a kitten."

"I did notice how quickly she came to you," I said. "You know, it's worth a try. I'll tell Bo about her."

Summer grabbed a tissue and sneezed into it three times. "I'm so sorry. My head is still drying up." She cleared her throat and shot me an inscrutable look. Was she blushing? "Anyway, I wondered if I could meet up with Bo sometime...you know, outside work hours."

Yes, she was definitely blushing. I clapped my hands in excitement and Ella leapt to the floor. "Are you saying you want to date Bo? I can totally set that up!"

Summer placed the kitten she was holding on the carpet and chuckled. "I'm glad you're so enthusiastic, but I don't know if he'd think of it as a date. I saw the way Tara looked at him. Didn't she fly in all the way in from California to see him?"

I waved a dismissive hand. "He's not into her anymore," I said firmly.

Summer's eyes lit up and an impish grin tugged at her lips. "You don't say. Tell me more."

ON THE WAY home from Summer's, I started feeling guilty for suspecting Dylan of being in the art fencing ring. Sure, he hadn't told me everything, but he hadn't maliciously lied, either. The least I could do was call him up and apologize.

He picked up on the first ring. "Macy! I'm glad to hear from you. How's it going?"

I gave him a brief rundown of my showdown with Isabella Rhodes, and he seemed horrified. "She acted so...normal, you know? Posh, but normal. She took one of my flyers at the oyster roast and said she wanted to come to the art show."

"Be glad she didn't—she might've robbed you blind," I joked. "But I know what you mean. She was sort of a regular at Barks & Beans. In fact, the very first time I saw her, she was talking loudly about Gerard and what a great golf instructor he was. She also brought up that rhino horn in Alice's office. It's like she didn't even care that she was pointing people to her close connection with Gerard or the art fencing operation. I guess she never dreamed she'd get caught."

"Hiding in plain sight," Dylan murmured thoughtfully. "So..." He drew out the word and I smiled, guessing what was coming next. "I know you've been through some trauma. How about unwinding with, say, a fantastic art show featuring some Hudson River School paintings?"

I didn't even hesitate. I was certainly due for some down time. "You know what? That sounds like the perfect way to relax. I'll see you Monday night."

Just as I was polishing off a bowl of chicken noodle soup for a late lunch, Katie Givens called.

"Would you be able to drop by Ivy Hill tonight?" she asked.

Bo hadn't told me it was safe to return to the spiritual center yet, even though the FBI had completely shut down the art fencing ring, effectively releasing Moreau's grip on the place. Still, I planned to stay well enough away until Bo gave me his final go-ahead.

"Maybe you could come by my place?" I suggested. "What did you want to talk about?"

She sounded excited. "Doctor Schneider and I have been talking, and guess what? He wants me to be the director of Ivy Hill. I wanted to run an idea past you, one that has to do with Barks & Beans."

"Okay, but I can't make any final decisions without my brother, since he's co-owner. Should he come over and join us tonight?"

She gave a prolonged *hm*. "I'd say not at this point. It's kind of a hypothetical idea I just wanted to get your take on."

"Sounds interesting. How about you drop by at eight?"

Katie agreed. As I hung up, I realized that even though Katie would've stolen my dog and sold him for money, I had to admit the entrepreneurial masseuse had a whole lot of pluck.

KATIE CAME BUBBLING in at eight. I offered her a chai latte, which she immediately accepted. We sat down at the table and Coal sat on his pillow, eyeing Katie warily.

She cupped the glazed pastel mug in her hands. "Remember how I mentioned that I wanted to modernize Ivy Hill? Well, Doctor Schneider does too. He's seen in counseling what a mess drugs are making of our county, and Jedi's public breakdown just brought it home. We're thinking we'd have enough room to open a drug rehab facility at Ivy Hill."

I set my cup on the table. "That's exactly what I heard Gerard wanted to do, too. How ironic."

Katie's lips quirked downward. "I should've paid more attention to him, but he was such a stalker, you know?"

"It's okay—trust me, Gerard was no saint. So how does Barks & Beans play into your plans?"

She rapped her nails on the table. "Dog therapy...or coffee therapy, I'm not sure which. All I know is that it's uplifting to visit your cafe. You and your brother are bringing all sorts of joy to this town, and I'd love it if we could work out a way to share that with Ivy Hill. I'll bet you've already been a huge boon to the shelter."

Summer had told me as much, so I nodded, distracted as I pondered ways to work dogs into a rehab program at Ivy Hill. "Okay. I'll tell you what. I'll think about it and brainstorm with my brother and see what we can come up with. You do have a beautiful place up there, and I'd like to see it succeed in really helping our community."

Katie nodded. "We'll return to the original vision for Ivy Hill—a place where people can come to lighten their burdens."

It had grown late by the time Katie and I said goodnight and she headed home. It hit me that despite all the danger I'd run into lately, I'd also felt some of my *own* burdens lighten since I'd moved home. I'd kept busy with the dogs and the cafe, so I was no longer spending every spare moment fixating on Jake's betrayal. Plus, I'd gotten caught up on Bo's life, even discovering that he'd been a DEA agent for years.

And it felt like I was making friends. Summer, Katie, and Dylan seemed to genuinely enjoy getting to know me. I hadn't felt so *interesting* in a long time.

I sat on my bed and stroked Coal's head. Although Gerard's death was tragic, it had brought this wonderful dog into my life. And Coal had subsequently *saved* my life when he charged Isabella in the garden.

I glanced around my room, with its worn wooden floorboards and blue-striped wallpaper. This used to be Auntie A's room—the place I'd run to when my feelings were in a jumble, or when I felt life was treating me unfairly. She'd always drop everything to listen to me.

There was no way I could've ever thanked her for all she was to me, but I still had Bo, and we were a team. Auntie A would be so proud that her Hatfield kids had once again joined forces.

As I stood to turn off the overhead light, my phone buzzed. I walked back and picked it up, but the number was unfamiliar, so I let it go to voicemail. Turning on my lamp, I picked up my psychological thriller novel again. My phone dinged with a message.

I put it on speaker and played it. The man's voice was humorous and teasing. "Macy. What a cute phone message. It's nice to finally hear your voice. This is Leo Moreau. Say, can you give your brother a little message for me? Tell him that he might've won this round, but ol' Leo doesn't give up that easy. Thank you, darlin'."

My heart sank as I texted Titan the news, then called Bo. Leo Moreau wasn't finished with us yet.

You can now preorder Heather Day Gilbert's

next Barks & Beans Cafe cozy mystery,

ICED OVER

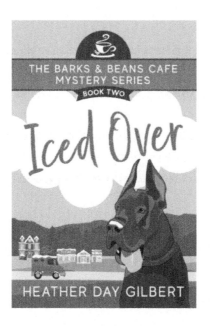

Welcome to the Barks & Beans Cafe, a quaint place where folks pet shelter dogs while enjoying a cup of java...and where murder sometimes pays a visit.

Black Friday turns fatal when an armored security truck hits an icy patch and runs over an embankment near the cafe. With one driver dead and the other in a coma, police are baffled by the discovery that $500,000 is missing from the truck's cache.

When strangers show up at Barks & Beans asking nosy

questions about a young cafe employee, Macy's mama bear
instincts kick in. She can't ignore what her gut is telling her—
that things aren't all they seem on the surface—and with a little
help from her brother, Bo, and her Great Dane, Coal, Macy
follows up on a few leads of her own. But if the ruthless thief
beats her to the stash, the thin ice she's been skating on might
just crack.

**Join siblings Macy and Bo Hatfield as they sniff
out crimes in their hometown…with plenty of
dogs along for the ride! The Barks & Beans Cafe
cozy mystery series features a small town, an
amateur sleuth, and no swearing or graphic
scenes. Find all the books
at heatherdaygilbert.com!**

The Barks & Beans Cafe cozy mystery series in order:

Book 1: No Filter

Book 2: Iced Over

Book 3: Fair Trade

Be sure to sign up now for Heather's newsletter at heatherdaygilbert.com for updates, special deals, & giveaways!

And if you enjoyed this book, please be sure to leave an review at online book retailers and tell your friends! Thank you!

Made in United States
Orlando, FL
03 April 2023

31674729R00146